YENOHAN'S LEGACY

<u>Previously Published Books</u>

Union Jack (2011)

Yenohan's Legacy 1ST Ed (2013)

Why Antarctica: a Ross Sea odyssey (eBook – 2015)

Being Lucy: the story of a recluse (2018)

Antarctic Engineer: memoir of John Russell (2019)

YENOHAN'S LEGACY

A HIGH COUNTRY STORY

Dale Lorna Jacobsen

Dale Lorna Jacobsen
PO Box 456
Maleny, Queensland, Australia 4552
www.https://dalelornajacobsen.com

Publisher's Note: This is a work of fiction. Names, characters, places, and incidents are a product of the author's imagination. Locales and public names are sometimes used for atmospheric purposes. Any resemblance to actual people, living or dead, or to businesses, companies, events, institutions, or locales is completely coincidental.

Book Layout ©2017 BookDesignTemplates.com

Ordering Information:
Quantity sales. Special discounts are available on quantity purchases by corporations, associations, and others. For details, contact the "Special Sales Department" at the address above.

Yenohan's Legacy/ Dale Lorna Jacobsen. – 2nd ed.
ISBN 978-0-6485786-1-1

Acknowledgments

A s with any book, there are those who have helped to make Yenohan's Legacy what it is. My thanks to Chas Reid who allowed me to gate crash the Kosciuszko Huts Association work party at Westerman's homestead back in 1999, and to then-president, Maurice Sexton, who drove me all over the Boboyan District to visit huts off the beaten track, and to Mary Sexton who planted the idea that the Aboriginal side of this story must be told.

My deep gratitude to Dean Freeman, Aboriginal Heritage Conservation Officer, Southern Aboriginal Heritage Section, Dept of Environment and Heritage, who advised me, and arranged for Aunty Margret Berg of the Wiradjuri and Wolgal Aboriginal Nations, and Aunty Rhonda Bamblett of the Wiradjuri Nation, to read an early draft. Josephine Flood's works on The Moth Hunters proved an invaluable resource tool.

Daphne and Colin Curtis welcomed me into their home to describe, first hand, the life of a cattle and sheep family who lived in the Mount Clear District. They, too, had their land resumed when Namadgi National Park was formed.

I wish to acknowledge the members of the Kosciuszko Huts Association who work tirelessly with the NSW Parks and Wildlife Service to restore and preserve our heritage.

Preface

This story is dedicated to the men and women who settled the remote country of the southern highlands of Australia and who, assisted by Aboriginal stockmen and women, took part in the annual transhumance onto the high plains each Summer in search of fresh pastures for their stock.

Little remains to mark their passing — broken fences, gravesites, piles of rubble beneath tangles of blackberries and hawthorn bushes, the skeletons of once fruitful orchards, weed infested garden beds — but occasionally a restored homestead or cattleman's hut surprises those who wander over the mountains.

This story, therefore, also celebrates the dedication of the members of the Kosciusko Huts Association who relentlessly battle bureaucracy and the elements to restore and maintain the wood, tin and bark structures that were once homes, and thus preserve the heritage of early settlers.

It also acknowledges the Wolgal people upon whose land this grazing took place, watched by the ghosts of their ancestors.

*****

Glossary and pronunciation

porcupine - echidna
peacocking - taking the best sites for homesteading and stock use
pisé - construction of rammed earth, straw and animal dung
wigging, crutching, dagging - trimming of wool for the comfort and
hygiene of sheep
snow gum and black sallee - the snow gums in this story are Eucalyptus
pauciflora (with multi-coloured trunks); black sallees are Eucalyptus
stellulata (with dark green and black trunks)

KHA - Kosciusko Huts Association

Naas - rhymes with 'mace'
Namadgi - the Aboriginal pronunciation, with equal emphasis on all
syllables, is preferred above the Anglicised pronunciation which
emphasises the middle syllable

Kosciuszko vs Kosciusko. Perhaps controversially, both spellings are in
current use. KHA added the 'z' to their name in 2004. Since this story
takes place before 2004, spelling without the 'z' is used throughout.

PART ONE

...

CHAPTER ONE

(2002)

I looked to the west. Blue-black clouds were swelling beyond the arc of jagged mountains, dwarfing them, and there was little doubt they carried snow. I combed the camp ground for fallen branches to feed my fire. Daylight was fading fast, adding pink frills to the edges of the clouds, when I heard the distant hum of a motor. Twin beams split the darkening forest then swept around the camp ground, picking out tree trunks, the pit toilet and my tent, before coming to rest opposite my camp. The diesel engine shuddered to a stop and silence returned to the forest. I heard the driver's door creak open and saw a man slide to the ground and place his fists in the small of his back. He stretched lazily, audibly. He nodded "G'day" as he walked to the rear of his Landcruiser. I responded with a brief wave then turned back to my fire. Territorially, I resented his intrusion.

Twenty minutes ticked past.

I glanced in his direction again. He was squatting over a small saucepan, stirring its contents. Perhaps, I thought, I was being antisocial — although a woman on her own in such remote country could be excused for being antisocial.

I called out to him: 'You're welcome to sit by my fire if you want to.'

'No, it's all right, thanks anyway. I'm turning in.'

He finished his meal, rinsed his plate, turned out his light and disappeared under the canopy.

Beyond the western peaks, thunder rumbled and lightning lit the clouds from within, but the storm hadn't yet reached the ceiling of stars flickering beyond the black sallee branches over my tent. I crawled into my silver dome and zippered the flap closed.

A deep silver frost came with the morning. I placed twigs in the fireplace and gently blew the coals, waiting for them to erupt into orange flames. There was no sign of life from the Landcruiser. I counted out the number of breakfasts until pay day, then divided my muesli into six portions and poured hot milk over today's ration.

Still no movement from the Cruiser.

I sauntered over to the pit toilet on the far side of the campground, detouring to sticky-beak at my neighbour's camp. It was deserted but there were breakfast bits and pieces packed in a box on the ground beside the rear tyre. He was obviously an early riser. The sun crept across the frost hollow robbing the tussock grass of its crisp silver coating. The mountains, freshly dipped in snow overnight, still hunched beneath dark clouds.

For three months I had been wandering aimlessly around the southern end of Australia, on the run from the heat and wet of the tropical Queensland Summer, seeking out the coolness that comes with higher altitude. The month before, I had drifted into the Australian Capital Territory to discover its National Park, Namadgi. The further south I travelled through the park, the more its rugged remoteness cast a spell upon me, and I knew I would be staying for some time, exploring, walking, unwinding. I had found a magical place with tussock-grassed frost hollows ringed by snow gum-clad mountains.

The Murrumbidgee River patrols the boundary of the park, waiting to collect the spring snow melt from the creeks and rivers that begin life high in its mountains. But they are in no hurry to deliver their load. They tumble into heavily timbered gorges, meander across wide grassy plains and trickle through black reedy bogs before surrendering their life-giving waters to the river.

Walking is one of the joys in my life, and I had spent most days in Namadgi as I did this one — packing a lunch and wandering over the boundless plains, filling my socks with burrs and my lungs with pure cool air. When I returned from my walk, the sun had already retired for the night with a chill close on its heels, and Mr Landcruiser had returned to his camp.

I noted the good quality leather boots, gaiters, and sturdy walking legs beneath sensible shorts. He smiled and continued with his task:

sorting woodworking tools and packing them into a knapsack. I stoked up the fire and added thick long-burning branches.

'Would you like to warm up?' I asked.

'Thank you. I could do with it tonight.'

Still dressed in shorts — I had reverted to the familiar comfort and warmth of trackies — he rolled a log next to me with his foot and rubbed his upper arms with the palm of his hands, then held out his hands to the flames. At close quarters, he appeared older than I had thought, probably in his mid-fifties.

'This is a top spot,' I said.

A long pause preceded his answer, as if he was considering his response.

'Yes, I always think so.'

Conversation didn't flow easily from this man. I watched a flame circle a knot hole in a burning branch, then lick along a ribbon of loose bark.

'So, do you come here often then?' I probed.

'Whenever I can get away, but only when it's quiet. It's not so pleasant when it's full of campers.'

The thought suddenly occurred to me that I wasn't the only one whose private space had been invaded. He nodded towards the clearing before us, intersected by a small stream working its way amongst grass-capped mounds of soil.

'In a couple of weeks this'll all be white with snow. It's truly beautiful then.'

We sat in silence as I turned his words into mind pictures, then I remembered his carpenter's tools, unusual gear for a bush walker to be carrying in a national park. It seemed we had something in common.

'I'm a woodworker of sorts,' I said. 'I make furniture and things.'

He looked sideways at me, eyebrows raised in a query. You get used to this when you're a thirty-something chisel-wielding woman. But he showed genuine interest.

'What timbers do you prefer to work with?' he asked.

I sang the praises of silky oak, Australian blackwood, Tasmanian myrtle and other favourites, then I asked what he was doing with carpenter's tools in a National Park.

'I belong to an organisation called the Kosciusko Huts Association. We restore old graziers' huts and homesteads so the history won't get lost. You've probably noticed them on your walks?'

'Yes, I have. I took them for granted, though, never thought much about how they got there. So, is that why you're here this weekend? To do some work?'

'Yes. We're working on Thompson's hut up along Grassy Creek. A few clicks up the track.'

I had been on the road too long. Sawdust was in my blood and I missed my workshop. My fingers itched to grip the smooth curve of a saw handle again. Perhaps if I concentrated hard he would ask me along.

It worked…

'We could do with an extra pair of hands, that's if you're interested.'

'You read my mind. I'd love to come, so long as I can be of use. What time will you be heading off in the morning?'

'If we get going early we can make the most of the daylight. I'll give you a call when I wake, if you like.'

There was no need. I was up, measure of muesli consumed, before the sun. I thought of giving him a call but realised I didn't know his name. With cold, stiff fingers, I brushed the frost from my tent, rolled and stowed it in the back of my car. When he emerged from his canopy, I was sitting in a patch of weak sun on the log barrier beside my car, warming my hands in my armpits. I walked over to him and offered my hand.

'Suppose we should introduce ourselves,' I said. 'I'm Fran.'

'Kelvin,' he said. His hand hadn't yet chilled to the morning and his handshake was firm.

We pulled out from the campground half an hour later, my old Subaru following Kelvin's Landcruiser. We didn't travel far, only about ten kilometres to the west, before we stopped at a galvanised iron and chain wire gate attached to a thick post. Kelvin swung it open, then locked it again after we drove through. I leaned out my window as he returned past my car.

'That's overkill, isn't it?' I said, nodding towards a padlock dangling from a heavy chain.

'It's to keep the pig shooters out. They'd trash the place if they could get in. They think it's great sport to take pot shots at these huts, especially if there's a light from inside of an evening.'

I had wondered about rifle shots I'd heard through the week. They had made me feel vulnerable.

We followed two wheel ruts over a series of low hills sparsely covered with stunted, twisted snow gums, then wheeled in beside three more utes parked amidst a clutter of saw-horses and tools, timber and iron inside a circle of huge old pine trees. I was mesmerised by a building, with gaping holes punctuating its front wall, squatting on the bank of Grassy Creek. On its eastern wall, two magnificent stone chimneys tapered towards the corrugated-iron roof which shone in its newness. I switched off my engine and stepped from my car, waiting for Kelvin to introduce me to the men standing around studying a pile of timber.

'Good morning. How's it going?' said Kelvin, then turned to me. 'This is Fran, she's been camping up at Mount Clear, and I thought she could be useful this weekend.'

He grinned as he added: 'It's okay, she knows how to use a hammer.'

They were a disparate group of men. I shook hands with Norman, a man in his sixties who smiled from under a floppy hat, exposing a mouthful of crooked teeth; Geoff, about thirty with the build of a man whose passion revolves around physical activities; and Mike, dread locked, fresh-faced and in his early twenties. It was obvious from the outset that Norman called the shots, everyone hung around waiting for him to make decisions.

'Where do you want me to start, Norman?' I asked.

'The wall between the living room and the front bedroom has most of its boards missing. Are you up for that?'

'Sure, no probs.'

He sorted through some second hand boards in the back of his ute, and drew ones of more or less equal width from the stack.

'You'll find the studs are as hard as the hobs of hell. They've been standing nearly a hundred years. It'd be better to drill before nailing the boards onto them.'

'Roger!' I flicked a salute to him, and saw the corners of his mouth twitch into a smile, although I sensed he felt uncomfortable with a woman in the crew, even one who did know how to use a hammer.

I placed my hand on the flaking red-brown paint on the front door and pushed firmly against its stiffness. It creaked open and I stepped into a dimly-lit room measuring, maybe, five metres by two. The echo of my footfall bounced around the cold walls. To my right a few boards, secured at one end by rusty nails, drooped at odd angles from studs rising from the floor. I peered through an opening in the centre of the internal wall, past a door made from vertical planks. Floorboards warped and twisted their way towards the far wall.

I turned back to the room in which I stood. This had obviously been the living room. Fresh mortar held the chimney stones in place and a row of empty wine bottles marched across a mantelpiece of pale timber that looked and smelt newly planed. Scorch marks fanned out from the fireplace opening. I began to feel that this had been someone's home – long, long ago; before bush walkers bunked down for the night to escape blizzards.

*****

(1908)

The hem of Nola's navy serge skirt brushed the roughly-hewn verandah boards as she approached the door, stroking her swelling stomach with the palm of her right hand. The words "Grassy Creek" stood out boldly in their freshly burnt blackness against the pale mountain ash shingle hanging above the door. Her horse, tied to the railing, snorted softly to itself as it bent to graze the wiry grass. Leaning past his wife, Roger turned the polished wooden knob and pushed the door open. The astringent smell from the fresh red-brown paint hung in her nostrils.

The ring of boot heel on wood echoed around the room as she entered the dimness then waited for her eyes to adjust. She saw that the walls were, as yet, unlined. New studs rose from the floor between the two rooms, awaiting their cladding. She crossed the room and walked through the open door, made from vertical planks, to her right.

Sunlight slanted through a small casement window, casting a crossed shadow along an iron-framed double bed. She sat on the edge of the mattress and bounced to test its spring. Roger set his wife's case down on one of two narrow stretchers jutting out from the end wall.

A flash of blonde hair followed red as a young girl tailed a youth, aged about twelve, in the front door and straight out the back door, keen to explore. Roger ignored them, and with his chin jutting forward, raked his fingers through his bushy black beard, anxious for his wife's approval. But she was still assessing her new home. She returned to the kitchen and offered a match to the kindling balanced, ready, in the fireplace. With both hands, she removed the black cast-iron kettle from its hook in the recess, crossed the room to the back door and called for her son to fetch water from the creek. The boy left his sister balancing on the smooth rocks midstream and bounded across to collect the kettle from his mother.

Nola then turned to face her husband and her eyes twinkled with joy. He read the acceptance in her face. She liked cosy huts, and this was indeed a cosy hut.

*****

'Do you want to hold them or drill them?'

I turned at the words, pulled back to the present. Kelvin had followed me into the house, cradling the boards for the wall in his outstretched arms.

'Oh, I'm easy. I'll drill if you like.'

I focussed on the wall with its missing boards. The left side of the door jamb leaned to the right. Kelvin followed my gaze and said: 'Each board will need to be cut to length.'

'Wouldn't it be easier to straighten the door jamb before we start cutting the boards?' I asked.

'It's best to keep it the way it is. We don't like to change anything, unless it's potentially dangerous. See, we don't know whether the building's sunk over the years, or whether Roger Thompson didn't have a good eye. It'd be a pity to make it straight if that's not the way he built it in the first place. Sort of ruins the integrity of the building.'

'I didn't think of that.'

We measured the length of the first board, then took it outside to the saw-horses to trim to length. I warmed as I worked and removed my jacket. I selected a drill bit from Norman's toolbox on the verandah and secured it into the chuck of the cordless drill. As Kelvin held the board in place on the wall, I leaned into the drill. Norman was right, the wood was like iron. Kelvin worked diligently and quietly, but it was a companionable silence which, not being good on small talk, I appreciated. We made a good team.

After an hour, Geoff looked in through the front door: 'Smoko!' We laid down our tools and went out into the brightness of the morning. On a small fire by the stream, the lid of a billy jiggled in a cloud of steam. I accepted a mug of tea from Norman and sat lizard-like on a large rock, feeling the warmth seep into my behind. Kelvin produced a plastic lunch-box filled with Anzac biscuits and passed it round. I dunked mine into my tea and sucked the sweet fluid through the hard biscuit.

'Hey Mike, you joining us?' Norman called over his shoulder. Mike waved his arm high without raising his head and continued working on some window frames.

'Ah, the folly of youth,' said Norman. 'He's an apprentice. Totally obsessed. Thinks he's got to work all the time.'

I took my mug and wandered off around the outside of the building. I stopped to admire the sash frames Mike was slaving over. Recognising the timber as red cedar, I bent to breathe in its aromatic smell.

'A damn possum's to blame for this,' said Mike, straightening the kinks out of his spine. 'It crawled down the chimney and then couldn't get out, so it thought it'd chew its way through the softest wood it could find — namely this frame! It didn't make it though, the ranger found the animal rotting in the corner when he was doing his rounds. Serves it right!'

I left Mike to continue with his window and wandered on. I was surprised to find even here, so far from anywhere, people had introduced niceties to their modest existence. A long time ago someone had taken the time and care to fashion a scalloped barge board that ran right around the building beneath the iron roof. It was roughly carved, I could see each knife cut in the silvery bleached timber.

Between carefully-placed river stones that encircled the building, filling the space between the ground and the outside walls, skink tails flicked back and forth in the sun. Four large flat stones formed steps to the back door. The entire eastern wall, with its two graceful chimneys, was also made from these stones. I closed my eyes and ran my hands over their smooth surface, warmed by the sun. Kelvin came around the corner to fetch me back to work and the real world. Our wall awaited us.

By the time the call came for lunch Kelvin and I had finished one side of the interior wall. It was far from attractive. Each board was blotched with the remnants of its own particular colour of paint. Rusty ghosts of old nails trailed from their holes. The sun had moved on from the rocks by lunchtime, so I sat astride a sawhorse and munched an apple. Kelvin made two tuna sandwiches and handed one to me. I thanked him. He smiled. As I ate, I listened to the joyful banter of this group of friends. They knew each other so well. It was the first time I'd noticed Geoff had a stutter, and it was quite a pronounced one. But the stutter took second place in my mind as he animatedly told stories — and he really enjoyed telling stories. Then he asked: 'What's a n-n-n-ice girl like you d-d-doing in a place like this?' The smile on Geoff's face told me he was playing with the timeworn cliché.

'Basically, I hate the heat, so I'm trying to outrun it.'

'And you live in Queensland!?'

'Yeah, it's silly, I know, but something ties me to the place. Probably because it's where I grew up and it's always been home. Every year I grumble and carry on. I can't work, I can't think, I can hardly breathe in the heat. This year I decided to pack my car and head south. I've been camping wherever it's cool.'

'Well girlie, I have to admit you know how to use a hammer. Are you into carpentry or something?' Norman asked, forking salad from a bowl, sucking an errant bean sprout between his lips.

'She makes furniture,' Kelvin said. I thought I detected a note of pride.

'How do you get on in Queensland? Isn't it too humid up there?'

'It does have its limitations. Winter time is fine, but it's impossible to glue delicate pieces in the Summer; and as for French polishing, forget it! Moisture gets trapped between the layers of varnish, then I get a bloom on the surface and have to sand back and start all over again. It really tries my patience. But the payoff is that the heat gives me an excuse to get away on holidays over the Summer.'

'Have you ever thought of moving to Canberra?' Asked Kelvin.

'Often. Your weather's perfect here. Lovely and dry.'

During the morning I had been wondering about the family who had lived in this house, so I asked: 'Does anyone know anything about the Thompsons?'

'Not a lot,' replied Norman. 'I do know that Roger Thompson and his two brothers built this place, then Roger brought his wife and their two kids here not long after the turn of last century. One of the KHA blokes is interviewing any of the old folk who are still kicking, trying to get a hold on who was who and what was what. Just about everyone was related to someone else in the area.'

Norman rose to wash his mug: "Come on. Time's a-wasting!'

Everyone rinsed their mugs and upended them on a rock to drain. We still had jobs to finish, and the day was closing in. Kelvin and I returned to our wall.

*****

The journey from the outskirts of Queanbeyan south to Boboyan would have been arduous for anyone, but for Nola Thompson, pregnant and with two young children, it was particularly testing.

For forty-five miles they had criss-crossed rivers, climbed heavily-timbered ridges, held the horses back from galloping down steep rocky slopes. It was uncomfortable whether she was riding side-saddle or jolting beside Roger on the wooden seat on the dray. They would shelter overnight in small huts built by other cattlemen but open for use by anyone passing through. Each morning they left them clean and freshly stocked with firewood, the unwritten law of the bush. On the final morning they scrambled through Pheasant Pass to emerge finally at the spot where Grassy Creek and Naas Creek converge: their new home.

Nola unwrapped a loaf of bread she had brought from Melvale and placed it on the table that filled the main room. She retrieved a tin of treacle and spread four thick slices with the golden syrup.

'Sorry our first meal isn't more of a feast,' she said.

None of the Thompson family complained. They were all eager to complete the chore of setting up home before dark and the rest of the day was spent between the house and the dray, transferring the pile of provisions, so necessary this far from civilisation, to the house. Joe carried boxes of kitchen chattels in to his sister, Ellie, who peeled the newspaper wrapping from each cup, saucer and plate and laid them out on the shelves nailed to the wall. Suitcases gave up their clothes, pots and pans, bed linen, all the multitude of furnishings needed even for a small home such as this. Because the house was nestled among the hills and mountains, evening shadows came early to Grassy Creek. By mid-afternoon the sun had disappeared behind the mountains and a chill settled around the house. In the fading light, Nola called her family inside. The heavy sacks of flour and potatoes that remained on the dray could await the arrival of Roger's brothers, Dan and Alec, who were following with the cattle and would arrive in a few days. Joe gathered fallen branches and worked hard with his axe, reducing them to firewood. Ellie collected kindling from beneath the black sallees behind the house and added them to the fire on the hearth.

The family enjoyed a simple meal of bread, corned beef and chutney then, wrapped in the warmth from the fire, listened as Roger relayed the stories and misadventures of building their new home.

'I hope you weren't expecting something bigger,' said Roger. 'When we were hard at work, I was proud of this place, but now that you're all here, I can see all its faults.'

'I can't see any,' replied Nola. And she really couldn't.

Roger pointed to a gap in the floor where they had run out of boards before they reached the far wall.

'We didn't split off enough boards to finish the job. And then there's the door jamb. It's crooked.'

Nola could now see how the door didn't quite meet the wall at the top.

'I should have fixed it; it'll always worry me, but I was just too exhausted by the time we'd finished.'

Nola looked around the room, appreciating each board that the brothers had split off from trees they felled during the Spring, in between mustering and drenching.

'Roger, I think you've given us a wonderful home. And no, I didn't expect anything bigger. This will do just fine.'

As the fire settled into a bed of glowing coals the children drifted to sleep, finally tired from the excitement of the first day in their new home. Nola moved closer to the candle and, opening her diary, wrote:

10 December 1908

We have finally arrived at "Grassy Creek" after a long week's ride. It is a lovely home. The men have done a grand job. I shall be very happy here.

*****

CHAPTER TWO

Nola lay beside her husband, listening to the sounds of the dawn chorus, so different from the bleating of sheep that had started her days until now. The smells that greeted her were different too. Pungent eucalypt, freshly sawn timber and last evening's wood smoke replaced the scents and smells of the well-established home that had belonged to Roger's family for generations. Only the aroma of Roger's pipe tobacco linked the present with the past.

In choosing to bring his family to Boboyan, Roger was carrying on a tradition of pastoralists who had brought their stock into the valleys surrounding Naas Creek every year since 1830; some staying for the Summer, others passing through on their way to the high plains of Coolamine and Currango further west, beyond the Brindabella Range. The Thompson brothers were no strangers to the area. Although their home was on Melvale, a moderately large station further north near Queanbeyan, they had travelled south each Summer for the past twenty years, driving their white-faced Herefords to the valleys that made up their forty-acre lease by Grassy Creek. At the end of the Summer drives Harry, their father, rode back to Melvale to care for his breeding stock, leaving his sons in charge.

But all that was about to change. Harry's back ached from years in the saddle and he no longer felt up to the week-long ride. Dan, who had joined the yearly trek when he turned twelve, learning on the job, was now sixteen and had proved himself a good horseman, so this year Harry remained at Melvale and let his three sons make the trip without him.

Harry had also seen the success of his fellow pastoralists who had taken a gamble and gone into wool, and he, too, had plans to bring sheep onto his property. For this, he would need to acquire more permanent grazing land. It made sense for Roger's family to move south to Boboyan permanently, build a home of their own, and extend the family's holding along the banks of Grassy Creek.

Until now, Nola had remained with her mother-in-law, Nancy, close to town and her children's school. She was aware of the special camaraderie that had grown between the three brothers during their long Summers together in a one-roomed pisé hut they had built fifteen years previously. Fibrous sheets of bark, stripped from stringybarks, made a good weather-tight roof above the walls of rammed earth and clay. They had planted a circle of fast-growing pines around their hut to block the winds, for the nights were cold, even in Summer. A fire, built in the stone fireplace in the end wall, was all the comfort they had needed.

With the first early-morning stirring of her children, Nola thought about their invasion of this formerly all-male world.

On the evening of the third day after their arrival, Roger said: 'I best be heading back to meet Alec and Dan. I'll leave at first light'.

Joe, lying before the fire, his head propped on his fist, turned to his father, waiting to be included in the trek. He was a good horseman, and he knew it, besides, it was a rite of passage for snow-belt youths when they turned twelve.

'Not this time, Joe,' said Roger. 'I'm sorry, but I think you'll be much more use here, given your mother's condition. There'll be other years.'

Rising before dawn, Roger farewelled Nola and the children and rode over Pheasant Pass to drop into the Naas Valley that would take him north towards Melvale, and the mob. Joe kicked a stone in disappointment.

*****

'Look at that, she can use a saw too!'

I paused, my left knee firmly planted on a plank across two saw-horses, my right elbow raised at the top of the pull of the saw. I peered at Norman, preparing to give him a lungful, then realised he was smiling at me. I relaxed my grip on the saw and stood upright.

'Why should that surprise you?'

'Actually, nothing about you surprises me. Oh, I know you probably think I'm an old fart and maybe I am, but in my world, women don't do this sort of thing, they leave it to their men.'

'I'm sure they're capable of it.'

'I'm sure they are too. It's not about strength: look at you, you might be tall, but you aren't exactly bulging with muscles. No, it's more about social conditioning. For some reason I expect a girl who does bloke's work to be butch. But there's nothing butch about you.'

'I'm not really the exception, you know.'

'Mmm … maybe.'

Norman collected the boards I had cut and took them in to Kelvin. I retwisted my long, fair, un-butch hair and pinned it out of the way and continued sawing.

At four o'clock Norman declared enough work done for the day and we cleared the inside of the hut, piling the tools and timber on the verandah. The mercury dropped and the air grew very cold. I pulled on my jacket and zipped it up against the wind. It was going to be a cold night.

'Are you sleeping in the hut tonight, Fran?'

I presumed Norman only asked me out of politeness, and I didn't wish to be seen as the girl guide gate-crashing the boy scouts' campout.

'It's all right. I'll camp outside, thanks Norman.'

'Don't take too long pitching your tent then, it'll be dark soon.'

I wrestled the wind for possession of my tent. Kelvin heard the flapping and ran to help. I threw him some tent pegs and we stretched the floor of the tent out between us, hammering the pegs into the compacted earth. When we'd finished, he pointed to the snow clouds rolling in from the south-west, much as they had done the night before.

'I'd say we'll cop it tonight. It's early in the season though.'

I thrilled at the promise of snow. I collected a crust of bread and my remaining tin of baked beans from my tucker-box and followed Kelvin indoors.

The hut no longer resembled a construction site. A fire leapt and crackled in the living room fireplace, and our three companions huddled close around it on their camp stools. A delicious smell rose from a bubbling billy dangling over the flames from a rusted hook.

After tea we sprawled, satisfied, around the room. The roaring fire had done its job, and relaxed into crimson coals. I lay on my side, my head propped on my knuckles, thoroughly content.

'That'd make a good damper fire,' I mused.

'I suppose you're good at cooking damper too,' said Norman.

'As a matter of fact, I make the best damper you'll ever eat.'

'Oh, is that true. Got any flour with you?'

'Of course.'

'Right!' He slapped his thigh as he prepared to make a deal. 'We'll give you a good fire in the morning and you can cook us a damper for morning tea.'

I cursed my big mouth. My skiting would rob me of my remaining flour. I had a satisfactory arrangement with the Australian Government. They paid me a small pension, enough to keep food on my table and bills paid. I owned my own house, life was more or less secure, but in the off-season of my furniture making, I only just got by with careful budgeting. The past month had been a balancing act between food and fuel. I did have a bag of flour, but only a small one, and it had to last until Wednesday. Then I struck on an idea.

'Tell you what. I'll cook a damper if you each give me two slices of bread.'

'It's a d-d-d-d-eal,' said Geoff. Norman foraged around inside his tucker box and held his payment out to me.

I'd secured enough food to last until pay-day. I felt smug. I looked over at Kelvin who smiled as if we shared a secret..

There was no hierarchy around the fire. Periodically someone stirred to place another log on the coals. Sparks sprayed, then died. The warmth of the flames, the friendship, and the wine, fed the stories each of these men told; perhaps they were trying to impress the newest member of the gang. None of the stories were wilder, nor more amusing, than Geoff's. Holding centre stage, he stammered his way through tale after incredible tale: abseiling down vertical cliff faces; hacking his way through the dense jungle in Northern Queensland with a tomahawk; scuba diving on the Great Barrier Reef. Most of his stories stretched the imagination, and the more excited he became, the more he fell over his words as he pranced around the room, acting out his adventures. His friends listened as though they didn't hear his difficulty. No one attempted to finish his words for him.

It was well past midnight when I yawned and bade them goodnight. The cold slapped my cheeks as I stepped outside the warm cocoon of the homestead. The roof glowed silver in the light of a waning moon in a sky unbelievably full of stars. I pulled my hood forward and hugged my coat across my chest as I scuttled to my tent. I kicked off my boots and wriggled into my sleeping bag, curling into a shivering ball, waiting for my body to warm the silk lining.

Sometime during the night I woke to a noise. My hair crept across my scalp. I lay perfectly still, holding my breath to heighten my senses, but all was quiet outside. Eventually, needing to take a breath, I relaxed and drifted back to my dreams. Then, in a daze of half-sleep, I heard it again: a mournful wail that passed from one voice to another along the ridge, heading north. The call had only faded a minute when it swelled again. It was singularly the most eerie sound I had ever heard. I knew it must be dingoes.

As they continued to wail, I began to hear the beauty in their song. The twenty-first century seemed far, far away.

*****

'What was that!'

Ellie sat up straight in her chair, her fork suspended midway to her mouth, her young ears straining, listening for a repeat of the noise that prickled the hair at the nape of her neck. But the only sounds were the crackling of the fire and the moaning of the wind in the pines. She resumed eating her meal.

A week had passed since Roger had left to meet up with Alec and Dan. The whole family wished for the time to pass swiftly.

'There it is again!' shouted Ellie. Fear gnawed at the pit of her stomach. She turned to her brother and mother with eyes as big as saucers, defying them to say they hadn't heard the unearthly noise.

Nola and Joe stopped eating and listened. Then they all heard it. Starting from the south, one wail passed along many voices until it reached the northern end of the ridge.

'It could be wild dogs,' explained Joe, shovelling his stew towards his mouth.

'Do you reckon they make that sort of noise?' asked Nola.

'Dad says they do.'

'Well I think they're probably wolves,' said Ellie. She had read of wolves roaming the forests in Russia, preying on unsuspecting travellers, particularly those with young children, and she wasn't

exactly sure of the distance between Russia and Grassy Creek. She gave an involuntary shudder: 'Make sure the doors are properly shut!'.

Joe checked the doors to appease his young sister, amused at the idea of a dingo trying to open the heavy doors.

Nola welcomed the family's move to Boboyan, but she knew the brothers' lives would now be very different, and spent the next day preparing for the men's return. She propped open the wooden shutter of the pisé hut with a stout stick and lifted her face to the breeze, then attended to the earthen floor, tramped hard and smooth over the years. She sluiced it with the contents of the morning's teapot to settle the dust, then swept the loose powdery top layer out the door with the tea leaves, using a broom she had made from ti-tree branches. The floor shone in its smoothness.

A fireplace, flanked by log benches, occupied the entire end wall. Nola shovelled out the built-up ash from the fire's bed then reset the fire. She looked up through the chimney, almost as wide as the fireplace itself, past the blackened rough stones to the sky beyond. Chimney design had come a long way in fifteen years, she thought, as she compared this with the brand new one in her own house not twenty yards away. Outside, she gathered fresh bark and headed for the ladder leaning against the clay wall.

'Here, let me do that, Ma.'

Joe took the sheet of bark and climbed the rungs of the ladder to repair the roof. Miffed at not being allowed to go with the men, he was determined to show he was capable of doing the work of a man.

He was very close to his mother and felt protective towards her. He was so like his father in his attitudes, although he had inherited his mother's red hair and freckled skin rather than the black hair and tanned arms of the Thompsons. As a four-year-old, he had watched his sister come into the world. Despite her independence Nola allowed her son to express his protective feelings for her during her pregnancy.

Late in the afternoon, as they were preparing to close the house for the night, the unmistakable sound of a mob of cattle moving along the valley filled the air: the barking of dogs; the shouting and whistling from the men; the cracking of their stock-whips; and the cloud of dust hanging in the air. Joe jumped onto Whisper, his bay colt, and galloped over the ridge toy join the mob. Roger was pleased to see his son riding towards him at full pelt. Pleased to be back.

Once the cattle were secured beyond the sapling gate, Roger dismounted and hugged his wife and Ellie. Dan removed his hat, shook his black curls like a dog and swung his sister-in-law in a circle.

'So, I'm to be an uncle again, eh?'

He winked at Joe, who was dutifully brushing the dirt and grit from the horses' flanks, and playfully swiped his hand across his nephew's head. Joe ducked and shadowboxed his uncle.

'You look after her, eh Joe?'

Alec, who was older than Roger by three years, didn't join in his younger brother's expressions of joy. He mumbled his greeting to the family as he stooped his bulky frame and disappeared through the door of the old hut.

The cattle would remain in the yards for a few days to settle down after the drive, then the gates would be opened to let them wander and graze at will until the next muster.

There were still provisions to be unloaded from the dray: the heavy sacks that had been left for the men to carry. They each grabbed a corner of a seventy-pound bag of flour and then dealt with the two-hundred-pound bags of potatoes, stacking them against the kitchen wall under Nola's direction. Roger looked around the room and screwed his face up. His home now resembled a storehouse.

'I suppose we need a place to put all this stuff.'

Then he turned to Joe.

'We'll start on that in the morning, eh Joe?'

*****

Nola was very pleased with their provisions hut of scavenged roofing iron, tied to a mountain ash frame with recycled fencing wire. A week later, wire cradles swung from the ceiling, depriving the bush rats of an easy meal from the flour and rice sacks.

Dan and Alec had ridden off to check on the spring growth of the grazing grasses — and to check on a few mates living on the slopes of Sentry Box Mountain to the west — leaving Roger and his family to settle in alone.

Nola enjoyed the process of turning their new house into a home. She and Ellie cut fancy patterns from old newspapers and, using a mixture of flour and water, glued the miniature paper curtains to the edge of the functional shelves. Ellie thought hers looked like snowflakes.

Nola sent Ellie to the provisions hut to fetch the bucket of tallow she had been collecting, stew by stew, over the past months at Melvale; scraping the fat from the tops of the stew pots, then rendering it on the stove until it turned pure white.

Nola also retrieved some old jam tins from the provisions hut to use as candle moulds, and tightly rolled torn pieces of cloth for the wicks. She pierced a hole in the bottom of each tin through which she pushed one end of the rag and secured it with a knot. She asked Ellie to hold the wicks up straight as she carefully poured melted fat into the moulds. She wrapped the free end of each wick around a twig and rested it across the top rim of its tin. They made six of them. Big fat candles that would smoke and smell, but would give enough light in the evenings to allow the family to read and Nola to sew.

While Nola had the tallow out, she made soap. Not soap for washing bodies, it was too harsh for that, but soap to wash their clothes, their dishes, and to scrub the floorboards. Nola emptied the remaining tallow into a laundry copper over a fire beyond the back door, then handed Ellie the pot stick with instructions to stir as she added Lux flakes, salt, caustic soda and lumps of resin from the trees. Then Nola went inside to make sure the candle wicks were still in place as the cooling tallow turned milky.

Every now and then Nola returned to the copper, took the pot stick from Ellie and watched how the mixture dripped from the point, then patted her daughter on the head and continued her chores.

Ellie stirred the pot. At first she was bored, but she started singing in time with the action and began to enjoy herself. Eventually Nola judged the brew was the right colour and consistency, and ladled the hot liquid into tin baking dishes. She stepped back to admire her first batch of soap, wiping the slippery residue from her hands onto her pinafore. It would need to solidify overnight before she could cut it into squares and store it in the wire cradles beside the flour and rice, away from the bush rats.

*****

I lay in my sleeping bag for the first few moments after I woke — before memories, anticipation and reality reclaimed my mind — mindlessly tracking the even stitching of the seam above my head.

The air was freezing, but the wind of the night-time had ceased. All was quiet.

I rolled onto my side and hugged my pillow. Soon the thought of my surroundings, the company of these delightful people and the prospect of a day's hard work filled the void. I unzipped my tent. A fairyland welcomed me.

The whole landscape had rounded into soft white curves that glistened with countless crystals. I drew this magic into my body as I retrieved my boots from the space between my tent and its fly and pulled them on. The new snow crunched beneath my feet as I walked slowly, heel then toe, taking in this new experience.

Isolated rocks, wearing white beanies, peaked through a fluffy doona of mist floating on the stream. Sedges dipped their snow-laden ribbons towards the water, and across the creek, the black and green trunks of the sallees stood stark against the white background. Each branch of the pines around my campsite bowed low beneath its load.

It doesn't snow in Queensland, at least, not where I live. I wandered around in the very early morning, delighting in each crisp footfall. I glanced towards the hut, pleased the chimney had not yet begun to smoke. Soon, the sun would send the long shadows of the mountains back across the plain and the world would waken; until then, I didn't want to share this moment with anyone. I sat on a rock and watched the mist waft and part. Tiny ripples radiated from the feet of insects skating across the surface.

The hut's rear door creaked open and I heard the laboured squeak of boots through new snow, followed by the trickling of water. I turned around. Norman was standing with his back to me, peeing against a low shrub. I watched, amused, as he carefully washed the snow off each leaf in turn with his golden stream. A sneeze caught me unawares. He stopped mid-flow.

'Oh! I didn't know anyone was up yet.'

He turned, quickly zipping his fly closed. I resisted the temptation to suggest he finish first.

'Have you ever seen anything so beautiful?'

I described an arc with my gloved hand in an attempt to diffuse the embarrassment.

'Only up here. Yes, it *is* special.'

'Are the others awake yet?'

'They're just stirring. Did the dingoes keep you awake?'

'No. That is, I did hear them, but they didn't worry me. Their call is quite lovely.'

'Not everyone thinks so. They used to scare the bejesus out of the early settlers. But you can't blame the dogs, they were only helping themselves to the meals the settlers provided. Meals-on-hoof instead of Meals-on-wheels.'

He chuckled at his own joke.

'G-g-g-good morning, Fran.'

'Morning Geoff.'

Totally uninhibited, Geoff walked to the same shrub and relieved himself, continuing the conversation over his shoulder.

'Nice of it to s-s-s-s-snow f-f-f-f-or you.'

Geoff shook off the drips, then zipped up as he turned around.

Smoke began puffing from the chimney, signalling the start of another day of activity. I collected my ration of muesli, tea bag and milk from my tucker box and went inside. Sleeping bags, pillows and blankets carpeted the floor. The empty wine bottles marched further along the mantelpiece. Kelvin handed me a steaming mug.

'Young Mike won't be up for a while, he over-indulged last night.'

I placed my hands over Kelvin's, feeling the warmth of his body as well as the tea. He kept hold. I held his eyes longer than the normal "thank you" time, then he slowly withdrew his hands from under mine. He wandered over to the window.

'Got your wish then?'

I followed and stood beside him, perhaps too closely, but he didn't move away. I noticed fresh snow around the rim of his boots.

'Have you been out already?'

'Oh yes. Mornings like this, you can't stay in bed. I've been walking since daylight. The year's first fall of snow is always the sweetest.'

I looked at him as he sipped the tea from his mug. His dark straight hair, neatly brushed, was turning grey at the temples — I hadn't noticed this before — and his chin was sprouting the beginnings of a motley beard. It suited him.

'Do you always wear shorts? Even in this weather?' I asked.

'Yes, I do. I hate having my knees restricted. Trousers get in the way when you want to jump over rocks and logs.'

Norman stirred the pot with a wooden spoon.

'Who's for porridge?'

Kelvin nodded in its direction.

'Go on, have some. It'll make your muesli go further.'

The hot creamy oats tasted good.

One sleeping bag writhed like a huge green caterpillar, and a mop of furry hair popped out from the top.

'Will youse all shut-up! Can't a bloke get any sleep round here?'

Geoff sat on Mike and tickled him mercilessly.

'Wakey, Wakey, rise and sh-sh-sh-shine.'

Mike sat in his sleeping bag with his elbows resting on his knees, his fair dreadlocks matted, his blurry eyes bloodshot and his bare torso strong and youthful.

'What time did you all get to bed?' I asked.

'Don't ask! Oh, my head feels like thunder.'

Norman passed him a coffee with a knowing smirk.

*****

Now that the horses were to be in the valley the year round, the men were kept busy cutting timber to build stables and a tackroom. The Thompson family owned twelve horses: a saddle pony and a pack-horse for each of them. Joe took on the care of the pack-horses. He had learned from his Uncle Alec that, to get the most from a horse, he must always appear calm and self-assured. Alec, although awkward around humans, was gentle and confident with his horse, constantly stroking him and speaking into the soft brown ear that flickered when it felt its owner's warm breath. Joe had noticed Dan's horse was always frisky and ready to bolt. A lot like Dan.

Joe rode off to explore his new territory. He headed east towards the foot of Mount Clear, ducking and weaving through the olive-coloured trunks of the black sallees that fringed the frost hollow. As he entered a stand of snow gums further up the mountain, Whisper's ears pricked forward. A breeze stirred the leaves, and all Joe could hear was their soft rustling, but Whisper's hide quivered beneath his legs.

Joe thought he saw movement through the tangle of silver and orange trunks, then he heard a soft snort — so did Whisper. Joe gently pulled on the reins and stroked the side of his horse's neck. Whisper cocked his left ear backwards, attentive to his master, but his right ear was focussed on the bushes ahead.

Again Joe saw movement through a gap in the trunks. The breeze passed Joe and parted the leaves revealing six horses. The stallion, not much taller than Whisper's thirteen hands, was entirely black with a long shaggy mane and a full tail that swept the ground.

Nearby, protected by a cluster of mares' legs, two golden foals flicked their short straw-coloured tails. The mares, unaware they were being watched, drooped their heads in sleep.

Whisper impatiently pawed the ground. The lead mare snapped out of her reverie and nipped the foals on their rumps. The mob took off up the mountainside through a narrow gorge that disappeared between two granite pillars: the stallion leading, his mares close behind, surrounding the foals as they galloped. Joe did not need to encourage Whisper to follow.

When they reached the summit, the horses dropped out of view down the far side of the mountain. Joe reined Whisper in and dismounted as the drumming of hooves grew fainter. They were both panting: the horse from effort, Joe from the thrill. He stroked Whisper's black muzzle to calm him.

This was the first time Joe had been on the mountain top, over five thousand feet up. He climbed onto a large grey boulder and looked back to the west, beyond the fringe of peppermint gums growing lower down the mountain, past the thickly-wooded Naas Valley, to the golden valley of his new home. Whisper, trained to remain still once his reins were dropped to the ground, waited patiently, one hind leg resting on its tip toe, his tail swishing at persistent flies.

Over dinner that evening, Joe told his father of his find.

'The bush horses. Yeah, they're devils to catch and tame.'

'Have you done that, Dad? Caught them and tamed them?'

The pale skin between Joe's freckles coloured with excitement.

'Could we do that?'

'We usually catch some when we're up here. They make good pack horses.'

'I'm sure the lad could go with you,' said Nola.

'I've every intention of taking him,' replied Roger through a clay pipe between his teeth.

'It's time we put his horse-handling skills to good use. It'll probably be in a couple of weeks, so we can break them before the muster.'

****

CHAPTER THREE

*T*he Summer of 1909 was a happy time for the Thompson family. It was the first time they had lived alone. Nola's pregnancy progressed smoothly and she had never seen her children more content. Joe flexed his young muscles. Ellie read books and made up stories in her private eight-year-old world.

At first Ellie remained close to Nola and home, much as she had done at Melvale, but as she eased into this different life, she began to explore further afield.

Bounding across the rocks in Grassy Creek, she discovered an enchanted land on the far side. It wasn't hard to find fairy dells and elf holes in the frost hollow full of spongy sphagnum moss and flowering buttercups, white purslane, silver snow daisies, bright yellow billy buttons. She threaded the blossoms into chains to weave through her plaits. She became the Fairy Queen. Her subjects were silvery striped skinks and exquisitely painted yellow and black frogs *that hid amongst the rocks and mosses of the gilgai. Ellie served them tea on silvery new leaves of candlebark gums — perfectly round and the size of elfin dinner plates. She hung the moss-covered granite table with streamers from ribbon gums.*

Grey kangaroos that grazed the plains became a fleet of prancing white horses to pull her carriage; bogong moths were her means of flight, lifting her on their furry backs to the top of Mount Clear, watching benevolently over Grassy Creek Valley. The scribbles on the bark of snow gums recorded the paths of their journeys.

She lay perfectly still among ferns in the damp gully, listening to lyrebirds mimic sounds that made up their world: the call of the rainbow lorikeet, the barking of the Thompson's dogs, even the chopping of wood. Ellie wasn't fooled though. She knew it was the lyrebirds, betrayed by a chorus of chuckles between each carefully practised verse of their song.

Ellie discovered more than fairies beyond Grassy Creek. She found a forest of ring-barked mountain ash that became a harbour of ships' masts. Not that she had actually seen a harbour of ships' masts, but she did own a picture book with an illustration of one. Removing her lace-up boots and tucking her ankle-length skirt into her cotton bloomers, she climbed these masts to watch out for pirates' ships and desert islands. Taking footholds from stubs of broken limbs, she climbed so high she discovered the sleeping hollow of a masked owl. She told it her secrets which, in its wisdom, it kept to itself.

During Summer, Ellie saw a small group of Aboriginal women and children camped along the creek near her home. The women sat cross legged in front of their bark gunyahs, laughing together as they turned a goanna roasting on a small fire. The children splashed in the creek, flashing water and white teeth to each other.

Ellie noticed a girl, about her own age, watching from behind the trees, but when Ellie waved to her, the dark form flitted away to the bark shelters.

*****

Yenohan pulled her possum skin wrap over her skinny shoulders as she squatted behind the trunk of the gnarled old tree and shivered in the early morning. Her inquisitive brown eyes followed the movements of the girl with hair the colour of tussock grass. She liked to watch the pale-skinned girl playing games; would have liked to walk out from her hiding place and join in, but her mother had warned her that the white people were not to be trusted, so she pretended she did not see the girl wave to her.

*****

The land claimed by the Thompson family lay in a triangle bordered by three creeks that enclose the twin hills of Boboyan and Pheasant. Nearby three other families, Robinsons, Swifts and Davies, who had "peacocked" the best sites along the banks of these creeks for their own use. Safe in their isolation from the long arm of the law that forbade grazing on common land, the families turned their cattle out onto the unclaimed scrub that lay between their leases. The stock, all securely branded, mingled and roamed over Pheasant and Boboyan Hills between musters. As Autumn approached, Roger called the families of Boboyan together for a brumby run. Within a few weeks they would begin mustering cattle for the long trip back north for the Winter and on to Sydney for market, and they needed to ensure there were sufficient horses for the job. A few spares to take to the horse sales wouldn't go astray, either.

The brumby runs were a community affair. These horses belonged to the mountains, so the people of the mountains shared in their capture and ownership. Early on the morning of the run, Nola heard the dogs bark the arrival of her neighbours in the house paddock. This was the first time they had visited Grassy Creek since her arrival.

Little clouds puffed from the mouths of each rider and horse to hang in the misty air as Nola crunched across the grass to greet them. They weren't all men either. Nan Davies was as good a horseman as her husband, John.

At first Nola took this flat chested woman — dressed in moleskin trousers and shirt, with short brown hair tucked beneath a broad-brimmed hat — for a man sitting astride her mount, and was surprised when a female voice greeted her.

'Hello Mrs Thompson. I'm Nan Davies. Your nearest neighbour from over the Pass.'

She pointed over her shoulder with her thumb.

'I've been meaning to come and say hello for some time now.'

Nan leaned down from the saddle and offered her hand to Nola who accepted the firm handshake.

'Please, call me Nola.'

Then Nan beckoned to a boy and a girl who were waiting nearby.

'These are the kids, Rebecca and Steven. Would you mind if they stay here while we go out after the brumbies? They won't be any trouble. Just put them to work if they get under your feet.'

Nan suspected Nola would have taken part in the brumby chase had she not been so large with her unborn child. Nola, for her part, had no doubt she would become friends with this no-nonsense woman. They were of an age, although Nan's angular face had seen much more of the sun than had Nola's.

Rebecca approached the two women. She was a soft child, caught between puberty and womanhood, who bore the attitude of being more comfortable around the home than on a horse. Steven was ten and knobbly kneed, and not quite old enough to take part in the run. He hung back, resentment pulling his face into a scowl. Stan Robinson had brought three of his sons along and Jack Swift stood beside his only son, Michael.

Nola watched the party head off towards Mount Clear, fanning out across the valley searching for the tracks of brumbies, wishing she could have taken part.

*****

Yenohan was sitting by the fire with her mother, Mooroo, when the men rode across the creek. The tall slim man with the big black beard, who she knew to be the white girl's father, waved to them. Yenohan lifted her hand to wave back, but her mother caught her wrist and forced it back down by her side.

'No girl! Look away. You must not wave to those men. They grab girls like you and take them away from us. Make them sick or give them babies with pale skin. Sometimes, they never come back. You've got to be very careful, especially when we don't have our own men to scare them off.'

Yenohan had noticed her mother and aunties were particularly nervous when their own men were away hunting the jar bon moth or mustering the white men's cattle. But her people had grown to depend on the tea and sugar and baccy the white men exchanged for help with mustering the white-faced cattle. And, once a year, the boss man killed a big cow and left it out for them to eat. Mooroo said this was a small price to pay for using land her tribe had wandered since the beginning of time . Yenohan stayed close by Mooroo's side.

*****

Joe led his father and uncles to the site where he had last seen the horses at the foot of the mountain. They found them gathered in their day camp beyond the frost hollow, and the riders approached slowly, not wanting them to run just yet. The stallion eyed the approaching horsemen with suspicion and nipped his mares into a canter. The wild horses followed their well-worn path to safe ground higher up the mountain. The riders followed at a distance.

Halfway up the mountain, at the entrance to a narrow gorge, Stan and John were waiting, hidden within low scrub. During the past week they had constructed two sapling wings that funnelled into the gorge. Each wing followed a spur for a mile and was well screened by bush. They knew the horses would come this way: their track ran right through the gorge. That morning, the men had blocked off its far end.

As the brumbies approached the concealed wings, Roger cracked his stock-whip. At full split — mares and foals up front, the black stallion at the rear — the horses thundered straight up the side of the mountain into the jaws of the trap set for them. The riders tailed the horses, growing closer with each stride. The stallion overtook his harem heading for the top of the mountain but Alec, on the left wing, cracked his whip and the horses veered to the right. Following instinct, the wild animals headed for the protection of a densely forested ravine.

The trees whizzed past in a blur as Joe gave Whisper his head. The wild horses charged through the thickest bush attempting to shake their pursuers, but Whisper skilfully found his way between the trunks. The Boboyan riders kept pace with the horses, steering them by the crack of their whips. Nan rode on the right wing, keeping level with Alec on the left, the horses between.

The horses broke through the bush, nostrils flared, breath rasping to be greeted by Stan and John who, upon hearing the approaching thunder of their hooves, sprang from their hideout. The wild horses, spooked by the sudden appearance of men, were left with no choice but to run between the two granite pillars.

As the last tail flew past, Nan dismounted and pulled hard on a rope. A sack, weighted by a thick branch sewn in the bottom, dropped to block the entrance. The horses circled inside the enclosure, trapped, looking for escape. Their eyes flashed fear and fury.

Alec took control. Selecting some of the quieter pack horses, he led them into the enclosure with the thirteen bush horses. The stallion eventually calmed, sending a message to the rest of the mob that began to relax as they sensed that their leader had lost his fear. But night was closing in. The riders rubbed down their saddle horses and hobbled them nearby, then fed their dogs and built a fire on the leeward side of the corral. They cooked a simple meal. Rolled in their swags, they talked until the adrenaline finally slowed in their veins, then one by one, fell asleep with their heads on their saddles.

The sun rose to find Roger and Alec quietly walking among the brumbies, beginning the long task of getting them used to humans. They blindfolded the stallion and mares for the trip back, knowing that if the horses couldn't see where they were, they wouldn't try to escape. They secured halters to all bar one: a chestnut mare they could not pacify.

'Let her go,' called Alec as he swung the gate open. 'There's always one rogue. We'll catch up with her next time.'

The rest of the camp ate breakfast and packed their saddle bags ready for the ride back down to the valley floor. Roger handed the reins of the two golden foals to Joe to lead out. Once they were far away from Mount Clear, they removed the blindfolds from the older horses. Now lost, they didn't try to escape.

When they returned to Grassy Creek, Alec put the twelve brumbies into the horse yard with the packhorses, then waited outside the yard for the wild horses to settle. Hours passed before Alec made his next move. He'd made his mark. He entered the yard talking constantly in a smooth, barely audible voice and approached the black stallion from the side. He gently laid a hand on its thick mane, talking, talking, constantly talking, never taking his hand off the horse, then worked his way to the ears, fondling, stroking the nose, the forelock.

He brought his whole body in contact with the horse and began to crawl over him, playing with the thick tufts of hair around the horse's fetlock. The stallion bent his head and grazed. Alec took the cue and crouched beneath, stroking the animal's belly. Nola gasped as she saw this.

'Is he some sort of fool?'

'Shhhh!'

Roger motioned to Nola, and everyone else, not to make a move or a sound. He had seen his brother work his magic many times. Wild animals trusted this man who was devoid of social graces.

Supper was a very happy affair around the Thompson's kitchen table that evening. They had secured twelve good horses which they would share evenly between the families. Not a bad day's work.

After dinner, Roger wandered outside to smoke his pipe. He saw Joe leaning on the top rail of the enclosure gazing at the stallion.

'He's too frisky for you, lad,' he said as he approached the yard, packing a fresh load of tobacco into the clay bowl with his thumb.

'I could tame him.'

'I don't think so Joe. Besides, he'll fetch a pretty price at the sales.'

Joe had learnt well from Alec. He slipped beneath the rail and approached the horse, following the same procedure he had seen earlier that day. Roger watched his son's confidence. Before long,

Joe was stroking the animal's neck. It lifted its head and turned towards Joe, snorting as if nodding acceptance.

Dan was to return to Melvale to help Harry through the coming Winter. This did not please Joe who mooched around on Whisper as the days shortened. Forced to leave his school friends behind when the family left Queanbeyan, he had transferred his affection to Dan. He shadowed his uncle, learning about horses, cattle and life.

*****

'Right, gather round.' Norman clapped his hands. With the start of a new working day, he became the boss again.

'Today we want to fix the flooring in the back bedroom. Kelvin, you could make a start on that. As soon as bugger-lugs here has cleared his head he can get on with the windows. I'll hang the back door then I'll probably crawl up onto the roof to …'

The sound of a motor vehicle interrupted Norman's briefing.

'Ah, that'll be Bob, he said he'd drop by this morning to see how we're getting on.'

A car door opened then banged closed, and a man in a khaki jacket stooped in through the front door.

'G'day. How are things going?'

He was the park ranger and knew everyone, except me; we were duly introduced..

'Welcome aboard Fran. Are you staying here long?'

'Only till tomorrow, then I'll be heading across the Alpine Way to Geehi. I've heard there's a good camping spot there by Swampy Plains River.'

'On the old airport, it's a great place to camp, especially now that the march flies have finished. Be careful on the road though, it's quite treacherous with this snow. If we don't get any more it'll be gone in a couple of days, but it'll still be slippery on the corners.'

Then he addressed Norman.

'The pig-shooters are about, make sure you lock the gate when you leave. A couple of walkers had their tyres spiked yesterday when they went up Boboyan Valley.'

'Why would they spike their tyres?' I asked.

'The walkers and pig shooters hate each other's guts.'

'It seems to me the pig shooters are doing everybody a service; nobody wants pigs around,' I said.

'Yes, they are, but they mess up the park something awful. Churn up the ground with their fat tyres, and their dogs kill anything that moves. This upsets the walkers who come for peace and quiet.'

I shuddered at the thought of coming across a couple of shooters and their dogs. Kelvin handed me a crowbar.

'Want to pull up a few floorboards?'

I'd hoped we would be working together again.

Two hours later Norman appeared at the bedroom door.

'Come and see if you approve of the fire, Fran.'

I checked the fireplace in the main room. No flame. Crimson coals.

'Perfect!'

Kelvin gathered the rotten floor boards, but knew better than to dump them on the fire until I had finished with it. I tipped half the bag of flour into my enamel basin that served as mixing bowl, wash-up bowl and face-washing bowl; added salt, sugar, and the right amount of water. I mixed it all with my hands then dumped it onto a floured sheet of alfoil in the bottom of my camp oven. Taking the spade that leaned against the fireplace, I carefully scooped out some coals, placed the oven in the centre of the remaining embers, then tipped the shovelful of coals onto the lid. Such a delicate operation.

'Twenty minutes,' I declared, dusting my hands.

We waited on the verandah, watching the sun turn the snow to muddy puddles.

It was intriguing observing the dynamics of this group of men. All through Saturday Mike's abilities as a carpenter had shone through despite his youth. Norman began Sunday by reasserting his position as organiser, but by morning tea I noticed that, as problems arose, he deferred to Mike; reluctantly at first, then with greater ease as his confidence in the young man built. Norman's life revolved around the preservation of these huts and the history that went with them. By Sunday morning, Mike had proved himself worthy in

Norman's eyes. I wanted to know more about the people who had lived here, so I steered the conversation in that direction.

'It's hard to imagine a family living here,' I commented.

'The house was only half this size when it was first built. Just two rooms, the front one and the bedroom leading off it,' replied Norman.

'Didn't you say there were brothers as well?'

'Yep. Apparently three brothers held the lease jointly. Originally they stayed in an old rammed-earth hut — it was in amongst those pines where you're camped — then one of them got pissed off with a woman and kids invading his space and he built a slab hut up on the slopes of Mount Clear. Word is he came to a sticky end.'

'How do you know so much about these families? It was all so long ago.'

'There's always a relative who wants to talk. Of course, they exaggerate the truth a bit, you've got to sort out bullshit from facts. They were crusty old blokes, tough as nails, especially the ones who lived up here all year round.'

'I suppose they were tough women, too.'

'Not so much tough as dedicated. They wanted to keep their families together. There was a family called Robinson over in the next valley, up along Naas Creek. Mrs Robinson lived there with her hubby and fourteen kids.'

'Fourteen! Don't tell me she gave birth to them up here!'

'Not the first three, but the rest she did.'

I remembered the one and only time I had given birth: sterilised white hospital; midwife and nurses in crisp uniforms; machines that beeped, dials that flashed, tubes, gas mask; and a specialist gynaecologist to catch my son as he slipped from my body. Perhaps, I thought, the human race has progressed too far.

Bob sniffed the air. 'Mmm. That smells good. What's cooking?'

'Aha!' I sprang from my camp stool. One of the earliest lessons I learnt in life was from my grandmother: when you can smell the scones, they're ready to come out of the oven. I went to the fireplace with Kelvin, Norman, Mike, Geoff and Bob close on my heels. I spread my elbows: 'Give me room!'

I hooked two tent pegs through the triangular handles of the oven and carefully lifted it from the fire.

'Aren't you going to t-t-t-est it first?'

I gave Geoff a look that clearly said: "Who's cooking this 'ere damper?" and removed the lid.

'Wow! She really can cook damper!' Exclaimed Norman.

A golden crust, criss-crossed with cracks, filled the oven. Although I had no doubt it would work, I was much relieved. I inserted a thin knobbly twig, which I had selected from the yard, through one of the cracks in the middle. It came out clean. I wrapped my damper in a tea towel.

'It's not ready yet. We have to let it rest for ten minutes.'

Back on the verandah, Norman told me more about the Thompson family.

*****

Nola called Joe and Ellie inside before the night grew any colder. She looked anxiously at the snow clouds.

'Could you get some more firewood before you come in, please Joe?'

She lifted the camp oven from the fireplace and removed its lid. A golden crust of damper sat atop the rabbit stew, absorbing the rich gamey gravy. The bending made her back ache. She straightened and rubbed it hard with her fists. Joe dropped the firewood on the hearth with a clatter and stoked the fire. Ellie lit the candle on the table, then set three plates ready to receive the stew. They ate dinner to the accompaniment of the wind whistling across the roof and the rise and fall of the dingoes' call.

'I hope it snows tonight,' said Joe.

Nola was sure it would. She was sure she didn't want it to.

Roger, Dan and Alec had taken the cattle north to Melvale, where they would add their mob to Harry's for the drive through to the Sydney sales. This year, Roger was to turn around at Melvale and head back to his pregnant wife. There was still a month before the baby was due, time enough to take Nola, Ellie and Joe back to his parents' place, close to the Queanbeyan hospital. This was Roger's idea. Nola would have preferred to remain in her new home. Having a baby was not a new experience for her and she was sure she could cope on her own. Or at least, that was the plan. Babies have their own agenda.

When the fire had warmed the little house, Nola, Joe and Ellie retired to bed. About midnight all became absolutely quiet. Nola knew what it meant. She rose from her bed and padded over to the window to watch the snowflakes flutter down. She had to admit it was a beautiful sight. The slightest breeze made the flakes flurry as though taken by a strong wind, but there was no wind now. The storm had passed. She felt her son at her elbow. She felt comfort.

'I hope your father's back at Melvale by now,' she said in a low voice, not wanting to waken Ellie.

'Oh, he will be, he's probably on his way back up here,' replied Joe. Then he looked at his mother.

'Shouldn't you be in bed?'

Nola put her arm around his shoulders. They returned to their beds. Just before dawn Nola felt her waters break, felt the familiar contractions.

'Joe!' she whispered with urgency.

Joe woke immediately and jumped from his bed.

'What's up?'

'Don't wake Ellie. I need you. The baby's coming.'

He walked over to his mother's bed.

'What can I do?'

'Probably nothing yet, but I needed to tell someone.'

She paused. Joe thought she looked frightened.

'Perhaps you could stoke up the fire.'

Joe looked young and vulnerable kneeling in the glow of the firelight in the pyjamas he had outgrown, his auburn hair tousled, rubbing the sleep from his eyes with the heel of his hand. He brought his mother a sweet cup of tea. From Nola's bed they watched the snow gum, its boughs low under fresh snow, turn from silhouette to tree with the coming sun.

Ellie stirred inside her blanketed cocoon as Nola gasped, taken unawares by a strong contraction. The girl raised her head, looked out of the window, then jumped from her bed. She, too, had been hoping for snow. Then she noticed that neither her mother nor her brother showed the slightest interest in the world outside. Joe took command.

'Get some warm clothes on, Ellie,' turning to Nola: 'I'll fetch Mrs Robinson'.

'Are you all right, Mummy?' Ellie snuggled into her mother's side.

'Yes, Ellie, but we'll have our baby with us before tonight.'

'Does it hurt much?'

'Only every now and then.'

Joe made sure his mother was comfortable, then pulled on his oilskin coat and collected his rabbit skin hat from a nail beside the door. His boots squeaked through the snow as he hurried to the tackroom to collect his saddle. The unseasonably early Winter, his father's absence, the dash for help for his mother, all filled him with excitement. He felt truly alive as he urged Whisper forward through the deep soft snow.

Nola was well into labour by the time Joe arrived back at Grassy Creek followed closely by Mrs Robinson riding side-saddle on her own horse. Joe could recall his sister's birth, but Ellie had no previous experience, except for cattle and dogs. Her hand looked very small as she stroked her mother's stomach. Betty Robinson, a matronly woman in her mid-forties bustled into the room.

'Hello m'dear. So, this little one wants out, uh?'

'Oh, I'm so glad to see you, Mrs Robinson,' said Nola.

The older woman hung her coat and woolly hat by the door and, opening a hairpin with her teeth, replaced it in her short strawberry-blonde hair. At her request, Joe filled a basin with warm water and placed it on the kitchen table. She vigorously washed her hands — upper arms flapping — then told Joe and Ellie to remain where they were while she entered the bedroom, closed the door, and attended to Nola.

'You forget how much it hurts, don't you,' gasped Nola between contractions.

*****

CHAPTER FOUR

Mike hovered at the door, not wanting to let the damper out of his sight. 'Isn't it ready yet?'.

I collected the parcel, feeling its warmth through the bottom, and inhaled deeply over the steam rising through the tea-towel. I broke the damper into six roughly even pieces, and we melted butter and golden syrup over the fluffy lumps.

'Speaking of chimneys,' I said, through a mouthful, 'I can't help admiring the beautiful stonework. Are these the original ones?'.

'Not exactly,' said Norman. 'They were just a pile of rubble when we started work on this hut. Mrs Anderson — who used to live here as a kid — had a couple of old photos, and she could remember how they were built. We found a stone mason over the Victorian border and he was able to use most of the existing stones to rebuild them. Cost six and a half thou, but what a work of art!'

Norman wiped the melted butter from around his mouth with the back of his hand. He missed a smear on his chin.

'Right. That's enough gasbagging. Back to work.' Then as an afterthought: 'Bloody terrific damper, thanks Fran'.

Bob took his leave, satisfied that we were following the National Parks' guidelines for restoring the building.

I cleaned out my camp oven and returned it to my car. Kelvin followed, waving the nearly empty bag of flour.

'Don't forget this.'

As we walked back to the hut, I noticed a strange sight overhead. Two circular rainbows filled the sky: an inner and an outer one that surrounded a weak sun. The sky within the inner circle was almost white. The next band was pale blue, but the intensity of the colour beyond the outer circle almost hurt my eyes.

Kelvin saw me looking up.

'Ice refraction,' he said.

'Wow!'

I shuddered in the eight degree morning as we returned to our work. The paper-thin bedroom floor boards were roaring in the fireplace.

*****

Roger rode the full length of Naas Valley accompanied by anxiety. During the past few days he had ridden long into the night, only stopping to rest his horse before pushing on beneath ice haloes that, experience warned, foretold a severe Winter.

The snow had arrived accursedly early. There was a rule in the snow belt: the stock must be out by the first week of May. He and his brothers had departed in the last week of April. Just as well, as it turned out. Any later and they would have been trapped.

As the sun passed its zenith, Roger topped the rise of Pheasant Pass and saw his home settled in a field of snow, smoke curling from the chimney, as if it had always belonged beside Grassy Creek. He dug his spurs into his horse's flanks and galloped down the slope.

Roger could see Nola waving in welcome from the verandah. He was a hundred yards from her when the bundle she was holding in the crook of her arm took the form of a baby. He dismounted and approached his wife, hat in hand. She held out her free arm to embrace him.

'Meet your son,' she said, as tears trickled into her smile.

Roger took the tiny bundle from Nola and, bending his forefinger, stroked the sleeping face. His son's head followed the knuckle, trying to suckle it.

'You'd better come inside while I fill you in.'

Nola had sensed Roger might be home this day and had made a seed cake in welcome. She poured boiling water from the kettle onto tealeaves in an enamel teapot and placed it on the table beside the cake, then recounted the saga of the birth.

'I'm terribly proud of you, Mrs Thompson,' he said when she had finished.

'You can be proud of Joe, too. He took charge until Mrs Robinson arrived. Then he stayed with Ellie till it was all over. It was a strange ordeal for her, one she won't forget in a hurry.'

A month passed before Alec Thompson returned from the Sydney sales. With his coarse black eyebrows drawn together, he studied his new nephew.

'A boy'll be handy.'

Then he disappeared into the old hut.

The family was just finishing dinner when Alec tapped on their door.

'Sorry to interrupt, but I need to talk to you outside, Roger.'

Excusing himself from the table, Roger followed Alec into the night air. It took a few minutes for Alec to begin speaking.

'I've been thinking; I'm going up Mount Clear and build myself a shack before Winter sets in. There's not going to be much room here now you've got another kid; besides, we need someone up there to watch the stock. Dan can have the place to himself. He'll like that.'

'Are you sure, Alec?'

'Yeah. Things are different now, what with your family living here. I'll be happier on me own.'

'If that's what you want, Alec. Me and Joe'll give you a hand to build it.'

'Thanks mate.'

Roger watched Alec return to the old hut that the three brothers had shared for so long, sadness weighing heavily on his shoulders. Roger knew Alec didn't like change. Knew that, in his own way, Alec was fond of his brother's family, but the constant buzz of children irritated him, and that had been why he had usually stayed at Boboyan over the winters.

'He's turning into a hermit you know, Roger. He'll end up spending his whole life on his own and won't care one iota about the human race,' said Nola, when Roger explained Alec's feelings.

'You're probably right,' said Roger. 'I've seen it happen to other blokes. They live off rabbits and share their huts with bush rats. But it's really up to him if he wants to live that way, Nola.'

'At least we can keep an eye out for him,' she replied.

The following week Roger and Joe took the dray to Cooma to lay in provisions for the approaching Winter. Alec joined them, he needed to eat too, then Roger and Joe rode over to Mount Clear and helped Alec build his slab hut.

There remained one last task to complete before settling in for the Winter: the trickleburn. Roger rode out into the grassland with Alec and Joe, flicking burning wax matches as he went. A flock of sulphur-crested cockatoos smelt the smoke and screeched their warning as they circled, then flew away. A herd of twenty kangaroos leapt ahead of the smoke, heading for safer ground. The grass burned for a few days, creating a scene of apparent devastation, but there would be fresh sweet shoots come the Spring. The kangaroos would return then.

*****

Yenohan felt the change in the wind as it blew through the gaps in her bark shelter and knew her father, hunting jar bon in the mountains, would feel it too and return to their camp. She kept watch all day. In the last minutes of daylight, Mudjingal appeared on the edge of the clearing, followed closely by the rest of the Wolgal men and older boys. He dropped a net from his shoulder and presented his haul to Mooroo. Yenohan sat cross-legged with her mother and the other women, learning how to roast the furry bodies of the bogong moths, then grind them with smooth cobbles from the creek and form them into flat cakes.

For weeks, everyone feasted on the rich bounty; even the camp dogs grew fat. Mudjingal, normally strong and wiry of build, spread a little in his belly, while the skin of Mooroo and Yenohan took on a luxurient sheen.

As the winds grew colder still, Yenohan gathered her possessions — sleeping mat; possum cloak; basket for gathering plants — ready to move from the high country down to the low country along the

Murrumbidgee. The camp dogs recognised the change in daily routine and grouped of their own accord.

As was their tradition, the men led the way along the well-trod pathways followed by the women, children and dogs.

They left their bark gunyahs beside the creek. They would most likely still be there when the moths returned next year, but if they weren't, they would build them afresh.

They followed the creek to the crossing below the homestead. Yenohan looked for the girl, and saw her climbing a tree beyond the far bank. Their eyes met, and the girl leaned out from the branches and waved. Yenohan looked towards Mooroo who was focussed on the track ahead. A smile spread across Yenohan's face as she lifted her arm slightly from her side and flicked her wrist in a brief wave.

*****

The sheep, when they arrived, took well to the valleys of Boboyan. With so much fresh grass, they roamed, heads down, grazing from dawn to dusk. They mingled with the flock of Stan Robinson whose selection sprawled along a narrow strip of land between Naas Creek and Boboyan Hill.

Stan, as lean and wiry as his wife was plump and soft, had brought his young family to the district fifteen years before. With a thin, hand-rolled cigarette permanently attached to his bottom lip, he had built a drop-side horizontal slab dwelling atop a small mound. He was particularly proud of the stone fireplace with its six inch thick mountain ash lintel. He concocted a mortar of soil and cow dung, bound together with hair from his mare's tail, to plug the gaps between the stones.

Then more kids came. When they numbered six, Stan extended the building lengthways by one room. When they numbered nine, he added another room. By the time his brood numbered eleven, he decided the building was long enough with five doors opening onto the verandah, and began another wing off at right angles, towards the south. He used weather-boards for the new wing and while he was at it, covered the deteriorating shingles of the original dwelling with roofing iron he had brought in from Cooma.

And still Mrs Robinson — as fertile as the soil that yielded an orchard from the seeds Stan planted — reproduced. He extended the vegetable garden, planted in strips, bordered by herbs.

This year, tired of the journey north to Cupacumbalong Station each Spring for shearing, Stan had built his own shed: just a two-stander, but the weather was kind and he and his Aboriginal stockman, Pullerkuinergong, sheared the complete flock in a week.

Six weeks later they found a suitable water hole in Naas Creek into which they poured Cooper's Powder, then dipped the entire flock in an attempt to protect them from lice and from the blowflies, whose maggots burrowed deep into the sheeps' flesh. When they had finished, Stan sent word out that he was about to kill a couple of cows and sheep. As was customary, neighbours gathered to share the feast. On the last Saturday of October in 1910 the Swifts, Davies and Thompsons arrived at Robinson's homestead to help with butchering.

A motley collection of black and white dogs were driven mad by the carcases hung to set overnight in a black sallee behind the shearing shed. Unable to reach the forbidden fruit swinging in a cloud of flies, they lapped at the pools of blood beneath. The butchers lay the best cuts aside for cooking later that afternoon and sliced the remainder into strips.

It seemed dogs and children were everywhere. Stan showed the children how to rub salt into the reserve meat and instructed them to climb onto the verandah roof to spread it on the blistering hot iron to dry in the sun away from the dogs. The strips would be packed into barrels when the sun had done its work.

The women scraped the skins of the slaughtered sheep, stretched and pegged them in preparation for sale in Sydney. Betty Robinson pulled the hide of a bullock over a fat tree stump to dry in the shape of a cask in which she would, ironically, store her tallow.

The smell of cooking steak filled the evening as the women charged the lamps with carbide and water and placed them around the walls of the shearing shed, then sprinkled the floor with sawdust and kerosene to make it ready for dancing.

Stan pulled the strap of his piano-accordion over his shoulder and, encouraged by the women, played every tune he knew many times over. The men and older youths gathered around the keg of rum he had provided, watching in amusement as the women and children danced and sang along to the familiar tunes.

*****

Joe and Dan had worked together throughout the day, up to their armpits in bloodied meat, but when they went to the wash-house to clean and dress for the evening, Dan discouraged Joe's company. Deeply hurt by this unexplained rejection, Joe sat outside the shearing shed in the crisp night and watched the frivolity within. Then he caught sight of Dan dancing with Rebecca Davies; they were in their own world, brown eyes fixed on blue as they waltzed to Stan's music.

In the eighteen months since the brumby run, Rebecca's body had matured and rounded. She encouraged her long brown hair to curl around strips of cloth as she slept each night. And it did curl. She looked beautiful this night in a new organdie dress with a blue satin ribbon tied around her waist. As Joe watched them dancing he knew he had lost his closest friend, and the hurt intensified.

The dancing didn't interest Ellie, she thought it a childish activity. Selecting a length of straw for a bookmark, she left her book on a bale of hay by a lamp and went in search of Joe. She joined him on a log and watched their mother, jigging to the music with baby James on her hip, playfully pull their father into the circle of dancers. Roger's long gangly legs would not conform to the fast jig. With a self-conscious grin, he returned to the keg.

*****

CHAPTER FIVE

The white snow of the morning was melting to a mud-streaked slush around the homestead. Kelvin handed me an egg and lettuce sandwich. I smiled my thank you and noticed, for the first time, a sadness underlying his quiet calm.

'Are you returning to Canberra this afternoon?' I asked.

'No. I thought I might walk through the valley for a few days. Clear the head — you know.'

I pictured walking through the valley with him, my head could certainly do with a good clean out. I left the thought dangling.

'Is the slab hut still on Mount Clear?'

It was Norman who answered my question.

'Yes it is, although it's in a sorry state. I'm about to put in a proposal to restore it next, seeing as it's connected to this building. We need to go and have a look at it sometime soon.'

'Why don't we take a look after lunch?'

'Good idea Kelvin. Who would like to come and see it?'

'I should be g-g-g-getting back,' said Geoff. 'Got lessons to prepare for tomorrow.'

'I need to putty in the glass to give it the week to dry,' said Mike.

Kelvin raised his eyebrows in my direction.

'Oh, you don't need to ask. I'll be in anything!'

'We should fit in the front of my ute then,' said Norman, and he rinsed his mug and plate.

Geoff came over to shake my hand. 'I'll probably be gone by the time you get back, so I'll say goodbye now. It's not often you get to meet a woman like you Fran. It's been a t-t-treat.'

'I'm sure there's a lot of us around.'

Geoff grew uncharacteristically bashful. 'Well, I'm actually engaged to one. She would've been here this weekend except she p-p-preferred to go rock-climbing.'

This was the first I'd heard of Geoff's fiancé. It didn't surprise me that he was engaged to an interesting woman, though. I hoped she could keep up with her future husband.

'Goodbye Geoff. I'll miss all you guys, and this wonderful house. I wish I lived closer, then I could come to more work parties.'

'Why don't you hang around and give us a h-h-hand next weekend? It'll be our last before Winter.'

'We'll see,' I replied. I wanted to move on to Geehi and see more of the high country before I headed home to Queensland.

Norman was waiting in his ute with the engine ticking over. Kelvin opened the door and I climbed onto the middle seat — only really wide enough to hold a child — then he squeezed in beside me.

'Pardon me,' he said with a smirk, as he slid his arm along the back of the seat.

'Reminds you of being a teenager at the flicks, doesn't it?'

It did. I even blushed as I had when a fourteen-year-old had spent a whole evening inching his arm along the back of my seat, only to have the film finish as he lowered his hand onto my waiting shoulder.

We followed two wheel tracks eastwards across paddocks of the aptly named Long Flat, but the tracks petered out when we started climbing Mount Clear. No one came this way any more.

Our heads jerked back and forth as the ute pitched over rocks and into holes. My knuckles paled on the panic handle. Kelvin dropped his right hand onto my arm and braced me.

Then we entered a stand of peppermint gums. Norman firmed his grip on the steering wheel and peered through the dusty windscreen, weaving his way through tree trunks, dodging logs half buried in the undergrowth. He appeared short-sighted. I hoped he wasn't.

My sense of adventure waned as we crashed through the other side of the forest to face the ground rising steeply past patches of unmelted snow which hid behind large rocks.

'Please, tell me you're not going to drive up there!'

Norman pulled on the hand-brake and turned off the engine.

'No, we walk from here.'

The view was spectacular. He reached across and removed a steel tape measure and notebook from the glove box.

'Some say Alec built up here so's he could keep an eye on his two younger brothers,' said Norman, pointing to Grassy Creek homestead, a mere speck far below. 'Others say he built here so's his brothers could keep an eye out for him.'

The first thing I noticed, as we approached the building, was the smell — like stables not mucked out for years. The vertical slab walls weren't in too bad a condition, but the roof was. Rusty iron partially covered the remains of fragile shingles, and loose sheets peeled back from the verandah, flapping noisily in a rising wind.

The verandah roof leaned to the left, balancing on thin saplings that, had they not been cut down nearly a hundred years ago, would have grown as huge as the orange and grey trunks behind the building.

The stink intensified as I stepped through the doorway. Sunlight, exaggerating the bleakness of the walls, forced its way through the gaps and spread on the floor in prison bar stripes. Overhead, pinpricks of light pierced the tin roof.

The source of the awful smell lay piled against the wall in the corner. Moist animal manure slowly rotted the split slab floor. Human litter was all around too — chip packets, drink cans, stubbies, plastic bags…

There were two rooms. I walked through into the second, dodging a tangle of cobwebs, and found the entire end wall missing. Beyond a primitive fireplace lay a pile of rusting iron that had once been a chimney. Oh, it must have been a bleak place in which to live.

'Here's something,' Norman called from the first room. I returned through the doorway and found him excitedly probing the wall.

'I can't quite read it. The light's not good enough.'

Kelvin produced a pencil torch from his shorts' pocket. I peered over his shoulder. In the circle of light was a very small piece of newspaper. Kelvin swept his torch around the rest of the walls, picking up other remnants in its beam: 'Might be some interesting reading here,' he said.

'Whoever lived here must have been a hermit,' I said.

'By all accounts, Alec Thompson was a recluse. He holed up here all Winter, hunting rabbits for food then selling the fur in Summer.'

'It must have been freezing,' I said.

'That's what these were for,' Norman said, flicking a loose scrap of paper. 'Sheets of newspaper can be quite effective at stopping draughts. He'd have been cosy once the snow built up and blocked off the gaps.'

Kelvin went outside and picked over the heap of chimney material.

'I reckon we could rebuild this without too much trouble,' he called through the missing wall.

'We could reuse this iron and get the framing from those gums over there.'

Norman ran his tape over the sheets of tin, measured the chimney opening, and made notes in his book.

I looked at the shambles. 'Do you reckon it's worth rebuilding?'

'You'd have said that about most of the huts we've rebuilt if you'd seen them before we worked on them. Thompson's wasn't much better than this when we found it. But if we don't do it, our heritage'll be lost,' replied Norman. defensively. 'Most of the damage to this hut's happened in the past ten years. We don't know if it's pig shooters or over-zealous greenies.'

It was my turn to be defensive. I considered myself a greenie. I hadn't seen Norman as a greenie-basher.

'What do you mean by over-zealous?'

'Some of the tree huggers reckon these structures have no place in a National Park. They know that if they wreck them enough, Parks will have them demolished.'

We walked onto the front verandah, treading lightly on the rotting floor. Kelvin pointed to the verandah wall, peppered with shot. 'Someone thinks all this building's useful for is target practice. What a bloody insult!'

Norman sighed. 'It really cuts me up seeing the old huts in this state. I'll take a few pictures and then we'll head back down.'

Kelvin and I waited on the verandah as Norman clicked his way around the building.

'It's so beautiful up here with the snow.' I wasn't sure if Kelvin was talking to himself or to me.

I said: 'I suppose you'd prefer to live up here. On your own.'

'Not permanently, I'd miss the human contact, but it'd be good to spend a season here, skiing down those slopes.'

Norman rejoined us, rewinding the film on the spool of his camera.

'Okay, that's all we can do here today. I've got enough to write a report. With luck, we'll get the funding to get the old darling back to her original condition.'

Halfway back to Thompson's hut, Norman pulled off the road. 'You might like to take a look at the remains of the old school house,

Fran. There's only the fireplace left now, but it was very important to the families that lived here. They put up a real struggle to get it.'

It took a few minutes to find the remains among the thick undergrowth. I looked around at the colourful trunks and thought what lucky kids they were to spend their school days here.

*****

When Stan took a break from playing, Nola sat on a plank, elevated between two bales, to catch her breath. But the children wouldn't let Stan rest for long, and dragged him back to his accordion. He sang along with his own playing, and the thin cigarette attached to his lip bobbed up and down in time with the music. His tattooed arms pumped the bellows; long spidery fingers danced over the keys. The raw magic of his music filled the air. Nola watched the children dancing the quadrille and their squirming bodies reminded her of the days, before she married Roger, when she had taught the children of Adaminaby School.

A seed of an idea wedged in her mind, then grew to a complete thought. She handed James to Roger and hurried out of the shearing shed and crossed the rocky paddock to the Robinsons' house. She burst into the kitchen where Nan was spreading thick slices of bread with butter from the crock. Betty Robinson stopped pouring hot water into a large enamel teapot as Nola's excitement tumbled out of her.

'I've been thinking. We should apply for a half-time school, right here in Boboyan.'

'Gosh, what made you think of that?' asked Nan.

'There are fourteen school-aged kids here tonight. It's ridiculous for them to have to ride all the way to Shannon's Flat every day and all the way back home again. I was a teacher before I married Roger. That may have been fifteen years ago, but I've still got the skills; I've been teaching Joe and Ellie their lessons since we came here.'

'Supposing you're right, how would we go about it?' asked Betty. Nola stopped pacing and leant her fists on the table.

'The first step is to write to the Minister for Public Instruction in Sydney. I'll do that. Then we'll need to fill in forms with the details of all the childrens' names and ages.'

Nola, aware that Betty could read but barely write, turned to Nan: 'Will you get those details Nan? You've known these people longer than I have.'

Nan placed the sandwiches she had been making onto a large wooden tray and handed it to Nola, then picked up another full tray herself. 'I'll do it tonight, Nola. You'll let us know if we can do anything else to help?'

The three women carried the supper to the shed, infected with Nola's enthusiasm.

The sky to the east was receiving its first blush as the families saddled their horses and dispersed with sore heads and sore feet and their share of salted meat.

Before she lay down, Nola sat at the kitchen table and wrote a letter with an appropriate amount of fawning for a Minister of the Crown:

To the Hon. Minister for Public Instruction,

Sydney.

Sir,

I most respectfully beg leave to make application to you to kindly take into consideration the necessity for having a part-time school in the district of Boboyan. This would be very convenient for several families living in the vicinity and there are already fourteen children who would attend such a school. I might inform you that this would save the children travelling to Shannon's Flat school, a distance of some seven miles. As many of the children are of a young age, you will see the necessity, if possible, of making some arrangements. I might also inform you that I have been a school teacher for many years, and would be pleased to accept the job, if it were offered to me, of instructing these children.

Trusting my application will receive your kind consideration.

I remain,

Your obedient Servant,

Mrs Roger Thompson

A week later, when the mailman arrived on horseback with their fortnightly mail, Nola handed him the letter to carry back to Cooma and send on its way to Sydney.

*****

Three weeks after writing to the Honourable Minister, Nola smelt smoke.

Roger said he had never known such a dry Summer as the close of 1910. Even the hardy snow grass suffered under a merciless sun that crossed the sky on its daily search for rain. The sheep, brought to the mountains to gain condition, were now losing weight.

'Surely they won't burn off this year?' Nola said to herself.

She propped James on her hip as she prodded the clothes in the boiler. Now eighteen months old and independent, he wriggled free and slid down his mother's apron to wobble off in search of his sister. He found her dangling her feet in a small pool, reading a book. He crawled onto her lap and pointed to the pictures with a moist finger.

As they retired to bed that evening, Nola saw an ominous red glow to the north-west. Come morning, grey smoke filled their valley. Alec and Dan appeared at Roger and Nola's door before they had finished breakfast, eager to head off and investigate the fire. They returned late morning with the fire hot on their heels.

'It's coming this way!' yelled Roger as he made for the provisions hut to gather hessian sacks, yelling instructions over his shoulder.

'Joe, open the gates and let the horses go.'

Roger tossed the sacks to his wife: 'Here, collect all the blankets in the house and soak them with these'.

Nola ran to the creek with blankets and sacks piled high in her arms and threw them into the water, stamping them under the surface with her feet. Joe released the panicked horses.

By the time orange tongues licked around snow gums to the north, the entire Thompson clan was armed with wet sacks, on the lookout for spot fires.

This wasn't a crown fire — not yet. Long ago, when the Thompsons had first taken up the lease, they had ring-barked trees in the hills near the house paddock to increase grazing land, and cleared undergrowth near their hut. They knew their home was safe, it was now simply a matter of keeping vigil until the fire front passed.

****

A hot Summer had forced the Wolgal people higher into the mountains. Crisp grass crackled beneath Yenohan's feet as she wandered the hills with Mooroo, seeking the daisy yam tuber and the starchy heart of the tree fern trunk. Her keen nose caught a whiff of smoke. There was little doubt it came from where the white men lived. Each year, they burnt more bush and animals fled in fear. Their fires were different from the ones the Wolgal people lit to flush out kangaroos to kill for food, they sometimes got out of control and spread over the whole country.

The smoke grew thicker as the sun grew hotter and Yenohan ran with her family back down the mountain to their gunyahs beside the creek. She only had time to grab her possum cloak and the basket that had taken her so long to make from the fibre of the kurrajong before the yellow flames appeared in the trees on the ridge. She knew what to do. The only means of escape was to crouch in the creek bed as the orange death roared overhead. Below the level of the bank, she would escape the choking smoke.

They were all safe, but their shelters sparked. The fire didn't differentiate between bark on a tree and someone's home.

Yenohan heard the cry of the roo dogs that couldn't outrun the flames. She thought she could hear every animal cry. And the earth cry. Mooroo pushed her body further into the shallow water as the worst of the flames passed overhead.

*****

Roger, Joe, Dan and Alec rode over their blackened paddocks. They couldn't find anything green or anything alive, not even their hopes. The whole day they searched for their sheep. Then they found them: two hundred curly black lumps huddled against the fence that had been built to contain them.

The men clung to the hope that the cattle had found refuge in the deep ravines.

*****

I held out my hand to shake Norman's, but he took it and enfolded it with his.

'Can't tell you what a joy it's been working with you, girlie. I hope you don't mind me calling you "girlie". To an old fella like me, you're just a slip of a thing.'

I withdrew my hand and hugged him.

'I don't mind at all, Norman. Thanks for letting me join your work party.'

He slapped Kelvin on the back of his shoulder, as mates do.

'And you take care, you old bugger. See you next weekend.'

Mike finished loading his tools onto the tray of his ute and waved goodbye as he climbed into the cab. Kelvin and I waved until their tail lights slipped over the hill and were lost in the twilight. It had been easy for us to pass secret looks and innuendoes back and forth whilst in company. Now alone, such behaviour seemed out of place and an awkward silence fell between us.

'I'll light the fire, eh?'

We built a fire near my tent, on an ash bed of countless past fires. The night was clear and crisp with not a cloud in sight, a far cry from the previous two nights. Even the wind had abated.

Silence is not so loud beside a fire, but I needed to know some facts about this man before I became any more attached to him, so I jumped in, boots and all, and addressed the question uppermost in my mind.

'How does your wife feel about you going away on your own?'

I thought he hadn't heard my question, as he kept prodding the fire with a long stick. Eventually, the stick became still and he answered.

'I doubt she even notices I'm gone.'

Not usually a bad judge of character, I had bet a considerable amount of emotional energy on the fact that Kelvin was free to respond to my gentle seduction. When I looked at him, he was staring at me, his eyes most serious.

'I wish I were free, Fran.'

Then he continued jabbing at the fire.

'Maggie and I have been married for thirty years. She's a good woman, but her world is very different from mine.'

'How so?'

'She hates being away from the comforts of her home; I can't stand living in the city. She needs constant company; I feel more at peace on my own…' he looked sideways at me again and the intensity gave way to a smile: 'or in good company.' Back at the fire. 'She belongs to the tennis club and plays every other day. She goes to restaurants, the theatre, you name it, she's into it. She's got her own circle of friends. Me, I need my space. I feel closed in at home. Our house is right in the suburbs of Canberra. In the early years, I tried to get her to come walking and camping with me, but it nearly drove her crazy, so I put it out of my mind. Once the kids left home I started doing my own thing again, then I joined the KHA and met Norman. He took me back into the outdoors. I owe him a lot.'

I hugged my knees, pondering the sense of duty that keeps couples together when children and love have moved on.

'It must be difficult to live together with such different attitudes.'

'Oh, you get used to it. We don't see that much of each other nowadays, we mostly pass on the front steps. Just lately, I've been wondering where my life is heading. That's why I want to walk up the valley for a few days. I've taken the week off work, told them I need a holiday.'

'What is your work?'

'It's pretty boring. I'm an office Johnny with the public service, like everyone else in Canberra.'

'That surprises me. I thought you'd have been an outdoors worker. Surely it would suit you better?'

'Oh yes! Many's the time I've thought of it, but Maggie and the kids needed the security that came with the job. And it was important when the kids were growing, but it no longer seems relevant. I look to the future and don't get excited by what I see. I've always scorned retirees who tend their roses, thought they should get a life, now I need to put my money where my mouth is, or I'll be joining them.'

'Surely your wife could have shared your passion some of the time?'

Kelvin shrugged his shoulders.

'It's not her way.'

'That makes me so angry! Selfish people demanding everything from their mates, and giving nothing in return!'

'She gave plenty. She was a loving and vibrant partner. And a great mother.'

I was rebuked.

'I'm sorry. Didn't mean to tread on any toes. But you say "was", not "is".'

'It's hard to see when change begins. One day, you wake up and there's a great gulf between you. You're not aware when it started to open up, but suddenly, you can't jump across.'

Then he straightened and the ruddy glow from the fire caught a smile spreading across his face.

'And what about you, Fran McMillan. Where do you stand in life?'

'Somewhere between birth and death.'

But I knew that wasn't fair. I had spent the last half hour questioning him. He deserved the same in return.

'I'm not the loyal type. Well, not any more. I was married for twelve years but felt suffocated. For me, life's too short to make sacrifices. My marriage was the loser.'

'Got any kids?'

'Yes, one. A boy, Nigel. He's fifteen.'

'Where's he?'

'America. He refused to leave his father when we split, so I lost them both.'

'That must have been hard on you.'

I don't like to lift the scab on old wounds, but the fire and my companion were comfortable.

'Yes, it is hard. You give birth to a baby, give them all your love and nurture them, then they're gone, leaving a massive boy-shaped hole. That was four years ago and I still smart over it. I'm trying to sort out my life too. All I know for sure is that I want to keep making furniture. It's the only thing that fulfils me.'

I tried, unsuccessfully, to stifle a yawn. I found speaking about myself boring, and I was bone-weary after the two days hard physical work.

'Why don't you go to bed, Fran. I'll probably sit here until the fire dies.'

'Maybe I will.'

I rose and reluctantly left the circle of warmth.

'See you in the morning.'

Kelvin smiled goodnight.

*****

Nola buried herself in never-ending chores while she waited for a reply from the Honourable Minister. When it finally arrived in February 1911, four months after she had written to him, the answer was brief in the extreme. It came with a form asking for more detail than Nola possessed: names and ages of each prospective student, and the character of the proposed building. Early that afternoon she rode over to enlist Nan's help.

Nan read the letter through a couple of times before dropping it in her lap and saying: 'I didn't know they'd want details of the building. We haven't even thought of that'.

The two women sipped their tea in silence, but Nan's mind was abuzz. 'I think we should hold a meeting and ask for help. Jack has had a hand putting up most of the buildings in the area. He's bound to have some ideas.'

The following Sunday the four families gathered around the Robinson's kitchen table, which groaned beneath a mountain of food, to thrash out the details.

John Davies had the first idea: 'You could use some of my land for the school'.

'We need to make it legal, though,' said Nola. 'You will need to prepare a lease for us all to sign and charge us a few pennies in rent. That should satisfy the department. I'll get that organised.'

'And what about the building?' Asked Nan. 'We need to have four walls for the kids to sit inside.'

This time it was Jack Swift who had the answer. 'The school at Tom's Plains closed a couple of years ago because they ran out of kids. I can't see why we couldn't use some of the boards and tin. It's no use to anyone the way it is. We probably only need to ask.' Jack knew the school well; he had built it when his son, Michael, had reached school age.

They all rode home in the evening, charged with tasks and enthusiasm.

Nola wrote to the Minister again, forwarding particulars of the children and requesting permission to use the materials from Tom's Plains school, then she patiently returned to the work of drenching, wigging and crutching new sheep the men had brought down from Melvale to replace those lost in the fire. It was a job Nola shared with Joe. When they had finished, Joe set a line of rabbit traps off into the scrub. There were plenty to catch.

*****

The shadow behind the snow gum grew into a girl. Ellie rose from the rock where she had been preparing the fairy's tea party and approached her. Ellie removed the wreath of sedge and flowers from her own head and nestled it amongst the dark curls: 'I crown you Princess… what's your name?'.

'Yenohan.'

'I crown you Princess Yenohan.'

Ellie took Yenohan by the hand and led her to a wombat hole nearby. She bent down and carefully parted the fine branchlets of she-oak curtain covering the entrance, then plunged her arm as far as it would reach into the miniature cave. When Ellie withdrew her arm, the most beautiful creature she had ever seen sat in the palm *of her hand. The tiny dress was made from salmon-coloured woolly ti-tree blossom, the hair that tumbled to her tiny waist was the silk from flowers of the reeds. Her lips were ruby red from wild raspberries she had eaten. Ellie spoke into the palm of her hand.*

'Tea is ready, Your Highness.'

Ellie gently laid the Fairy Queen on a small seat she had prepared for her. Two tiny slippers peeped from the scalloped hem of the floral dress as it spread over the glistening granite. Ellie guided Yenohan to another rock, and the two girls took up their positions either side, serving the Queen. A patchwork gold and chocolate butterfly landed on the table to observe, and stayed. Mud pies were served with sand cakes and wild raspberries.

Yenohan didn't understand the white girl's magic, but she knew it came from her mind. She fondled the plaited crown on her dark hair and giggled with Ellie as she drank make-believe tea from a make-believe cup before their make-believe Queen.

'What's your name?' asked Yenohan.

'I'm Eleanor, but you can call me Ellie.'

When Yenohan showed her mother the circlet of sedge and flowers, Mooroo turned it over in her hands, admiring the fine work, but knowing it was not of Wolgal making.

'Have you been to the white man's house?'

'Only to the creek nearby. Ellie gave it to me.'

'Ellie?'

'Ellie said I can keep it. She is my friend.'

Mooroo handed the crown back to Yenohan. She had feared this moment ever since the day she saw the two girls make eye contact. Her fears could not possibly include such a young person.

'Well, don't you go talking to any of the men.'

Now that contact had been made, the two girls often sought each other's company. Ellie showed Yenohan her secret spots amongst the gilgai, but was surprised to find Yenohan already knew her yellow striped frogs, and could climb trees faster and further than she dared. Ellie read stories out loud to Yenohan, pausing, as she turned each page, to point to the accompanying picture. It pleased Nola to hear their giggles as they flung flour about her kitchen in damper-making frenzies.

Ellie, Joe and James now had their own bedroom — a lean-to with wattle and daub walls that Roger had built out the back next to the stairs. There, Ellie dressed Yenohan in her prettiest clothes.

One day Ellie ran to the tree where they usually met to find Yenohan's camp deserted, their fires cold. The Wolgal tribe had moved back to the low country for the Winter.

*****

CHAPTER SIX

Each Summer, as Yenohan's family returned to the mountains, they found more sheep spreading out over their land, and there were new huts to house the men who watched the sheep. This year, as they trod their old pathways through the land, they heard rifle shots warning them to hurry through.

The first task for Yenohan and Mooroo was to replace the bark on their shelter. Mudjingal had left the day before to hunt jar bon. At first Mooroo could not place the strange rumbling noise, although the sound of galloping horses was familiar enough. It grew louder, closer, coming from the direction of the track used by the white people. Now close enough to see, it took the form of a wagon upon which sat men in uniform — one white man and six Aboriginal men she had never seen before — who sprang from the wooden deck before the horses came to a halt in the clearing around the fireplace.

Yenohan emerged from the gunyah to see what the fuss was, and one of the policemen made a grab for her. She pulled away and ran towards the creek, but when she looked back over her shoulder, she saw Mooroo being hauled onto the wagon. Yenohan ignored her mother's screams for her to run to Ellie's house and raced back to the mayhem; she was more terrified of losing her mother than of the red-faced policeman with a bulbous nose who grabbed her arm. This time, she was unable to pull away. Bundled onto the splintery deck, she curled into Mooroo's side. Together, they watched helplessly as the white policeman struck a match on the sole of his boot and threw it into their gunyah, then laughed as he leaped onto his seat and flicked the reins over the horses' backs.

*****

Ellie was plucking caterpillars from cabbages in the house garden when she heard the screams coming from Yenohan's camp. She began running towards the creek, but was overtaken by Nola who turned to face her daughter, barring her path. Ellie dodged to the right, then to the left, arms flailing, trying to get to her friend to see what was wrong. Nola kneeled before Ellie, holding her wrists, endeavouring to calm her.

'It's okay. Yenohan'll be looked after.' But Nola knew the emptiness of her own words as the wagon rumbled its way north to Edgerton Mission Station hundreds of miles away.

Throughout the afternoon, Ellie sat on the creek bank surrounded by smouldering gunyahs, trying to understand why Yenohan had been taken away with her family. At dinner time, Roger tried to explain: 'A lot of people want to use this land for their sheep, and they don't want to share it with people like Yenohan.'

'But that's not right! This is her home!'

'I never said it was right, Ellie, but it's what the government wants.'

*****

The Inspector from the Department of Public Instruction felt a certain reluctance to visit the Boboyan country. It lay in a remote corner of his district twenty-five miles from his office at Adaminaby. The trip was arduous and would take him away from his home comforts — and he particularly liked his home comforts — for the best part of a week. Longer if the weather was unkind.

He put the trip off as long as he could, but when his Chief Inspector ordered him to investigate the application for a half-time school, he could procrastinate no longer.

Inspector Amble was not, therefore, in a good mood as he heaved his portly body onto his pony and headed north in early April. Dressed, as always, in a three-piece woollen suit and tie, he wheezed and sneezed along the track as the dust, stirred up by his horse's hooves, hitched a ride on the dry south-westerly winds. He was relieved to stop overnight at Shannon's Flat before the long haul up into the mountains.

Shannon's Flat school impressed Inspector Amble. It boasted a student roll of nineteen children and had not long been granted the status of a full-time school on his recommendation. He availed himself of the hospitality of Mrs Smythe, a fussy lady of advancing middle age who laid claim to nearly half the children at the school, who insisted the Inspector stay at her home when he was in the district. He had little doubt this improved her standing in the community. He spent the evening listening to Mrs Smythe give her reasons why Shannon's Flat school should not be robbed of the Boboyan children, and thus be relegated to half-time status.

Between surreptitious sips from his whisky flask, the Inspector nodded agreement with the good lady and leered lasciviously at the young school teacher, who boarded with Mrs Smythe, bent over her needlework in the yellow glow of a kerosene lamp.

His spirit was as empty as his flask the next morning when he hoisted himself onto his long-suffering pony and resumed his journey northward.

****

Excitement accompanied the Boboyan families who gathered at Thompson's homestead early on the day of Inspector Amble's visit. Nola had prepared the children's bedroom, placing a fresh towel at the foot of one of the beds, and a vase of flowers on the lowboy. She allowed Joe to sleep in the old hut with Dan, and made up a pallet for Ellie and James on the floor of the main bedroom.

A morning tea of fluffy pikelets and warm scones was spread, waiting, on her best tablecloth when the Inspector shouted his arrival above the barking of dogs. He left his horse for Joe to wipe down and stable, then walked into the living room. He seemed to fill it. They all rose to greet him.

'Here, let me take that for you, Inspector,' said Roger, relieving the official of his bag and placing it in the leanto bedroom.

'Would you like to freshen up?' Asked Nola, offering a damp washer and towel.

Amble hawked the accumulated mucous from his sinuses then spat into his hanky which he refolded along the ironed creases and tucked into his trouser pocket.

'Yes. It's a devil of a long haul up here.'

He was in a better frame of mind as he wiped the fresh cream from his moustache with a linen napkin. He spread his fingers across the peaks of shirt peeping from his waistcoat, and belched loudly.

'Now, to business,' he said, and opened a folder onto the table. His audience perched on the front of its seats, expectantly.

'You say there are fourteen children of school age here, Mrs Thompson.'

'Almost. Perhaps not quite.'

'I've studied the papers you sent, and can see that there are six children of school age within a radius of three miles of the proposed site, and a further two within two miles. One of those children (I believe he's yours, Mrs Thompson?) is fourteen years of age and his attendance is only guaranteed for a further twelve months. Looking *at the ages, it seems to me there would be just five children in attendance come next year.'*

'The rest of the children live further away, Inspector, but our school would be much closer for them than Shannon's Flat,' Nola argued.

'Them kids's mine!' Put in Betty Robinson. Her ample bosom wobbled with her anger. 'It's not fair to expect them to ride seven miles there every day, and seven miles back again. They leave before daylight in the Winter — it's often snowing — and they don't get home till after dark. They're not much use round the place by then!' She folded her hands and defiantly tucked them beneath her bosom.

Inspector Amble filed this information away in his mind.

'Do you have a building?'

'Not as yet...' It was John Davies who replied. He had rolled his sleeves down over his long hairy arms and buttoned them at the cuff in honour of the occasion. He had also trimmed his bushy moustache, following the line of his full top lip. Nan thought her husband handsome.

'...but I've offered my land as the site, and we've asked for permission to use stuff from Tom's Plains school. It's been closed for a few years, and the desks and blackboard and easel are lying there, not being used. And we could use the building materials.'

Amble shuffled some papers: 'Yes, I see that on your application. How would you access these materials if permission were granted?'

'We'd take the drays over and load them up. I've built most of the houses round here, so it'd be no trouble to me,' said Jack Swift. 'We'd all pitch in and it'd be up in no time. Soon as you give us the go ahead.'

The heads all nodded in agreement.

'We'd better take a look at the site then,' said Amble.

The land was full of snow gums and granite rocks, but it was flat, and after wandering over the site for some time, Inspector Amble could find no objections.

Nola didn't sleep well that night, mostly because of the sonorous snoring coming from the guest in the children's room but partly due to her nervous hope for a succesful outcome.

In the morning, as Amble worked his way through three lamb chops and two fried eggs, Nola scanned his ruddy face for a clue as to his decision. But he showed no emotion as he slurped his tea then pulled the starched napkin from his collar and scrubbed the yellow yoke from his bristly moustache. He wiped the sweat from the back of his neck before heaping the napkin in the puddle of grease left on his breakfast plate.

Nola watched him disappear over the rise. She would have appreciated a word of thanks from her house guest.

A month went by before the mailman handed Nola a letter with an imprint from the Department of Public Instruction.

Dear Mrs Thompson

Subsequent to your application for a half-time school at Boboyan, Inspector Amble of the Department of Public Instruction has reported there would be insufficient children to warrant the opening of such a school at the present time. It is noted that a full-time school accommodating some nineteen students already operates at nearby Shannon's Flat.

Chief Inspector

Department of Public Instruction

Adaminaby

Nola fumed. She paced the kitchen, remembering how Inspector Amble had taken advantage of her hospitality, all the time knowing he would reject her application.

She picked up her pen, plunged it deep into the bottle of ink, and scrawled a reply that left the Chief Inspector in no doubt how it felt for young children to travel such a distance on a daily basis, and that it was of no concern to her that opening the Boboyan school would affect the numbers attending Shannon's Flat.

Her words reached their mark. A month later she received a further letter from the Chief Inspector, explaining that he had been misinformed by Inspector Amble, and granting the residents of the Boboyan District permission to access the remains of Tom's Plains school to complete their half-time school. And if she still desired the position, the Department would be pleased to appoint Mrs Roger Thompson as resident teacher.

*****

The people of the Wolgal tribe found themselves relocated among different language groups; the lingusitic and cultural differences between Wiradjuri, Ngunawal, Wolgal were of no concern or interest to the Aboriginal Protection Board. All blacks were rounded up indiscriminately.

They couldn't call this new place home. Home was down by the Murrumbidgee, living in bark huts they built themselves, or at their summer camp by Grassy Creek, not in these miserable boxes made entirely of tin where they baked in Summer and froze in Winter.

They had been used to spending their days catching fish, porcupine and possum. Now they were handed flour and tea, even clothes, from the ration store and told to till the fields in readiness to plant their first crop of potatoes.

Mooroo and her children were installed in a two-roomed hut while Mudjingal was away droving in western New South Wales. Yenohan, as the oldest child of her family, helped Mooroo turn their pitiful house into a home. They lined the tin walls with old hessian sacks, onto which they glued newspaper with a paste of flour and water. Yenohan cut patterns from the newspapers to hang from the edges of the shelves, as she had seen done in Thompson's kitchen. Mooroo sprinkled the dirt floor with water and began the daily task of sweeping it smooth.

Mr Hockey, both station manager and school teacher, lived apart from his charges. His house was warm in Winter with two fireplaces, and the wide verandah afforded coolness in Summer. At the rear of his house was a kitchen that, for two days a week, became a classroom. Yenohan and her four brothers crammed into the room with the other children to learn their lessons.

When the wind whistled through gaps in her tin walls, Yenohan lay on her palliasse and thought how warm it must be inside the manager's house with its thick stone walls.

The soil warmed with the approaching Summer, and men planted the first crop of potatoes. Rains came and the tops grew green and lush.

*****

I crawled from my tent into a deep frost, disguising slush untouched by yesterday's sun, and tripped over a small cardboard box. But there was no sign of Kelvin.

I unpacked the contents of the box: half a dozen eggs, a couple of tins of sardines, some powdered milk and bread, and a note:

In case you need it.

Cheers, Kelvin.

His knapsack and walking gear had gone, together with his hiking tent. The Landcruiser was locked.

I studied my map and found there were two huts further along Naas Valley; Horse Gully Hut, the most distant one, was fourteen kilometres from Grassy Creek. I guessed Kelvin would stop there for the night. I thought of sharing this gentle man's company for a few days, and packed my pack.

I smiled to myself as I quickened my steps after his. He had the key to the gate's padlock with him. I crossed Pheasant Pass and headed east.

The beginning of the track passed through wide plains that I had come to know so well over the past few weeks. I looked at Mount Clear further east, promising myself I would climb to its top one day. The heavy pack felt good on my back as I lengthened my stride and followed the track curving away to the north.

Signs of human habitation were everywhere, once I looked for them: a horse pound that had belonged to a long-gone homestead; deep axe-bites on ring-barked trees; yellow cement survey posts; old fence posts in the clutches of rusty barbed wire and blackberries.

I thought of the families who had called this place home, then had to move on when it became a National Park; I thought of my ancestors, cast out of their highland homes in Scotland by the English who coveted their grasslands for their own sheep; I thought of the Aboriginal people…

A wedge-tailed eagle soared effortlessly overhead scanning the ground for prey.

I crested a small hill and, leaving the wide grassy plain to the eagle, descended into narrow Naas Valley that wound its way between two mountain ranges, each thickly clothed in multi-coloured snow gums.

For the next couple of hours I walked up and over numerous ridges that separated small creeks. They all fed into Naas River which, in turn, tumbled towards the Murrumbidgee with its yearly flood of melted snow. Granite boulders sparkled in the sun.

I left the path and slid down through sedges to the river. As I scooped water to drink, little fish fanned out from my hand and hid beneath pond weed. I splashed my face to freshness and moved on.

Hunger was starting to nibble when I came across an arrow of stones in the middle of the fire trail. Above the arrow, a brown sign pointed:

TO DEMANDERING HUT

I followed the arrow and threaded my way through scrubby sallees. Grey fantails fluttered through the branches, displaying their tails, warning off the two-legged intruder. Demandering was a tiny hut made from corrugated iron. Each huge corner post (once a tree) had been squared with an axe above floor line to enable the tin walls to sit flat. Inside, I could almost touch both sides by stretching out my arms. It was just large enough for a fireplace and an old kitchen table which held a green plastic lunch-box centre stage. With the smell of many years' fires in my nostrils, I prised the lid from the lunch-box and found two fresh rounds of tuna sandwiches.

'Thanks Kelvin.' I consumed them with a smile.

The hut was so basic. I looked out the small sash window, past the rusting water tank, and questioned the improvements humans feel compelled to make in their lives. It had taken just a hundred years for humans to change from needing a sheltered place to sleep and a bolthole for bleak weather to demanding huge houses with a bedroom (and often a bathroom) for each person. In many ways I envied the shepherd to whom this place would have been home for months at a time. I would happily have moved in for the Summer.

After lunch, I continued along Naas Valley. It was only a few kilometres to Horse Gully Hut, but the knowledge that Kelvin expected me removed the urgency from my journey. I loitered by the river for a long time, letting my muscles unknot and my mind relax.

Fairy wrens twittered through a dense thicket of woolly ti-trees lining the river. I picked some yellow buttercups and white purslane and poked them through my buttonhole, breathing in their musky perfume, and continued along the track. I fell into an easy rhythm and delighted in the space my head found. The unmistakable smell of a campfire somewhere ahead wound its way through peppermint gums whose fine stringy bark looked dull against the glowing orange of the candlebarks. High above, a pardalote pipped its call, then disappeared into a hollow left by a fallen branch.

I walked on and the valley pushed its way into the foothills to my left. A large applebox, growing out from a field of wiry grass, spread its branches protectively over the charred remains of a cattle yard.

Horse Gully hut came into view and with it, the source of the campfire smoke. Kelvin was sitting on a log by the fire, grinning, and dangling the padlock keys in mid-air.

'You looking for these, by any chance?'

He stood to replace the keys in his pocket, waited for me to drop my pack, and wrapped his arms around me. I was weary, and leaned heavily against him for a few moments. Then he held me at arm's length and smiled.

'Gee, it's good to see you, Fran McMillan.'

'I wasn't sure if you wanted me to follow; that is, not until I found the sandwiches.'

I rooted around in my pack and handed over his empty lunch-box.

'Yeah, well, I thought you might need some sustenance on the way.'

'I'm not that badly off for food! But it was a lovely thought. Thank you.'

He turned back to the fire and stirred the contents of his billy.

'Why don't you put your pack in the hut?'

Horse Gully Hut was also a tin hut, but larger than Demandering. I noticed Kelvin had set two places at the roughly hewn table pushed against the wall.

'You were confident I'd turn up, then,' I said from the doorway.

'Not at all. That's why I left some food with you back at camp: in case you decided to wait at Grassy Creek till I got back,' he picked up the billy, wrapping his handkerchief around the handle, and carried it into the hut. He spooned braised chicken onto each plate: 'but I wanted to have dinner prepared, in case you did show up'.

'It smells good.'

'Just freeze dried, but it'll do the job.'

We ate our dinner by the light of the candle Kelvin had found on the table. I wiped the gravy from my mouth.

'Why did you leave so early this morning?'

He looked at me for a long time, with his habit of considering his answer before speaking.

'I wanted to give you the choice. I knew if I asked you to come with me, you'd feel obliged to tag along.'

'So, you really did want me to, then?'

'Yes, I did.'

I hid my smile as I left the table and walked outside to sit by the fire. He followed.

'How long's this hut been here?' I asked.

'It replaced an old mud hut that was built way back, around 1900. The stockmen used to stay in it when they passed through the valley, but it was damaged by fire. Same fire that got those cattle yards back along the track. Damn shame! A bloke called Roseby built this one to replace it around 1940. Then in the fifties, the Curtis family purchased all this country for extra grazing land. Their homestead used to be near Mount Clear campground, where you've been camping for the past few weeks. You would have passed the old horse yards at the beginning of your walk?'

I nodded.

'They lived here in these huts during mustering: mum, dad and four kids. All they would have lacked was privacy.'

He yawned: 'But right now, I need to hit the sack. It's been a long day'.

I made moves to extract my tent from the bottom compartment of my pack.

'Don't bother with that. Not when there's four walls offering.'

In the glow of the candle, Kelvin laid his sleeping mat on one of two wire stretchers, spread his sleeping bag on top, removed his boots and crawled in, fully dressed.

He raised his head and called out to me: 'Blow the candle out when you've finished, will you Fran?'.

He rolled over, and almost immediately soft snoring drifted out to where I sat by the fire. By the time I had laid my mat and sleeping bag on the other stretcher, there was very little of the candle left to burn.

If the dingoes howled that night, I didn't hear them.

*****

Nola's life was enriched by the challenges that came with teaching at the half-time school. She carefully planned each day's lessons and, aware that the parents of her twelve charges spent most of their day tending stock, taught not only the essentials of the English curriculum, but extras they would need in order to survive so far from urban society. Boys and girls alike learnt to sew a fine seam and read a recipe book, hone an axe and set a rabbit trap.

James, pretending to be a schoolboy, bent over his desk, his black unruly curls framing the slate as he drew stickmen while the older children scratched their times' tables. Joe sat at his lessons for twelve months, but Nola could see that, with her son now sixteen, there was little she could add to his education and that he longed to be riding the plains with his father and uncles, moving cattle and sheep around to the best pastures. When the time came to drench the cattle along Horse Gully, to spread salt in hollowed-out logs and wait for the iodine-deprived beasts to come to them, Nola finally agreed to release Joe from his school days. The work was physically hard, and Joe's lean body thickened as he helped pour drench down the throats of full-grown bullocks to protect them from internal parasites, then held the cleanskins for their sides to be marked with the sizzle of the Thompson brand.

During the weeks it took to complete their tasks, the men camped in a one-roomed mud hut in Naas River Valley, walled in by Booth and Mount Clear Ranges. Once a week, between teaching school lessons, Nola took provisions to her men, leading a packhorse up and over the ridges that separated smaller creeks. Ellie followed on her new red roan gelding, Freckles, with James sitting behind, clinging to her waist. Joe wasn't alone in changing from childhood to adulthood during this year. Nola noticed her daughter, who had been born with the new century, exhibit the first signs of womanhood in her thirteenth year. Ellie's curves were filling out and her face had lost the extra little chin from beneath its jaw line.

When the October sun chased Winter from the district, Joe joined the drive north for Melvale and shearing. In the three years since the fires of 1910, the flock had regained its size and strength, and buyers were now paying a healthy price for their clean, strong wool. Already missing his companionship, Ellie watched her brother ride north with the sheep.

*****

It came as no surprise that Kelvin had rolled up his swag and was tucking into breakfast by the time I surfaced; nor that, again, the landscape glittered with frost.

'Hope you don't mind an early start, Fran. I find it the best time for walking.'

'No, not at all.'

I took a mug of tea from Kelvin and wrapped my gloved hands around it. 'Thanks.'

I ate my muesli and stowed my gear into my pack.

'You'll need your tent tonight. There aren't any more huts from here on.'

*****

The ewes on Pheasant and Boboyan Hills were due for crutching, but a blizzard had been raging for a week, making mustering impossible, and Roger feared for the lives of his stock. Early one morning, he rode with Joe and Dan to the foot of Pheasant Hill to met up with Alec riding down from Mount Clear. The plan was to fan out, looking for the sheep, but the horses, already spooked by the wind, sank to their flanks in the powdery snow and the men had to dismount. They tethered their horses to some trees and continued on foot. Snow covered shrubs, rocks, logs in one soft blanket so that, with each step, they didn't know if they would settle on firm ground or fall through to their waists, legs entangled in branches of low vegetation or worse, down a wombat hole. The men knew they should not have been out in such a storm, but the ewes were in danger of freezing to death unless they were brought into the bottom paddock for lambing.

Roger shouted into the wind that whipped snow into his face, stinging his cheeks and blinding him: 'I'll take the northern side of Pheasant Hill; Dan and Joe, take the southern side. Alec, you check out Boboyan Hill. We'll meet up at the house paddock at lunch.'

Hour after hour Roger climbed over the hill, searching behind rocks, beneath trees, the dogs bounding ahead sniffing the snow for any signs of sheep. He found one ewe frozen, eyes open. Two sheep lost, including its unborn lamb.

Roger reached the top of the hill as Dan and Joe arrived from the south. The dogs were the first to find the sheep in a snow-walled prison of their own making at the top of Pheasant Hill. As the blizzard intensified overnight, the ewes had circled tighter and tighter and the heat of their bodies had melted the snow underfoot until they were treading bare dirt, trapped within a three-feet high wall of snow. Without human intervention there would have been no way out for these dumb creatures who would have eaten the wool off each other's backs to survive.

The men raked a break in the snow with their hands then stamped a ramp up and over the wall to lead the sheep out. They continued tramping back and forth, compacting the snow with their boots, creating a pathway for the sheep, leading down to where they had tethered their horses. They then rode the horses back and forth, continuing to ease the way for the string of bedraggled ewes that cautiously followed, two abreast.

It was long after lunch when they finally arrived back at the house. They shut the ewes in the relative safety of the paddock and went inside to warm up by the fire. They shed their oilskins and stripped their drenched clothes, hanging them on a line above the fire. Nola poured each a mug of hot broth. No one bothered that Alec wasn't at the house. He rarely came down from the mountain these days, so Roger assumed, as he collapsed into bed, chilled to his bones, that his brother had returned to his own hut. But tired as he was, he could not sleep. He turned to Nola, pulling her from sleep: 'What if Alec's still up there?'

'That's not likely, is it? Anyway, listen to the wind, it'll be the death of you if you went back out. Alec's no fool, he probably didn't find any sheep and he's gone back home.'

Roger wished he were religious, then he would have been able pray that his brother was safe.

The storm had lost most of its fury by morning when Roger went into the yard to check on the sheep. All seemed okay, but as he looked to Mount Clear, the usual wisp of smoke was absent from Alec's chimney. He threw open the door of the pisé hut, waking Dan and Joe.

'Something's happened to Alec, he's not in the hut.'

He strode to the tackroom and added a blanket and shovel to his saddlebag as he set out for Boboyan Hill with Dan, Joe and the dogs trailing behind.

Any tracks left by Alec were buried beneath yesterday's snow, but they knew the route he would have taken. Halfway up the hill they found Alec's horse still tethered to a tree. It was a wonder the animal was still alive. The men left their own horses and, taking the shovel and blanket, continued on foot, knowing the worst lay ahead.

Slowly they slogged on up the hill, sinking deeply with each step, calling for Alec, but knowing he would not answer.

This time, they did not spread out but remained together for support and strength.

It was mid-morning when the dogs, racing on ahead, stopped to paw at a flap of grey oilskin flapping like a flag from a mound of snow beneath a tree. Roger pulled the dogs back. They whined. Removing his gloves, Roger scraped the soft snow, slowly uncovering the coat that covered his brother's frozen body. He sat down beside Alec, tears filling his eyes, guilt filling his heart. He had known last night, as he lay awake, that he should have made sure Alec was at his hut. Joe and Dan sat beside Roger. Dan brushed the snow away from Alec's unseeing eyes and closed the lids. Joe placed a hand on his father's shoulder and left it there.

Roger wiped his eyes with the back of his hand and rose to pick up the shovel. 'We won't know how this happened just by sitting here,' and he gently began to release Alec from the snow. It wasn't until he reached Alec's foot that they found their answer. A tree root, growing around a rock, had left a gap just wide enough to swallow an ankle, and wouldn't let go, even when Alec's struggling had worn through his flesh to the bone.

They lifted Alec's body onto the blanket. Dan and Joe took the corner with his feet, Roger cradled Alec's head in his end of the blanket, and they made their way back to the horses.

The piteous party arrived back at Grassy Creek just on dark, with a very worried Nola pacing the verandah. They all lifted the blanket-wrapped Alec from his horse and laid him on Ellie's bed. Dan set off for Cooma to fetch the constable. There was no need for Nola and Roger to speak of their decision of the night before. Both knew how the other was suffering because of it.

****

Alec's passing brought changes to the dynamics of the Thompson household. Dan moved in to the two-roomed hut on Mount Clear and Joe moved from boyhood into the old pisé hut.

When Ellie's chores and lessons were finished for the day, she escaped into her world of books. Joe was away from home more than he was present and James held little fascination for her: she found his four-year-old games tedious. Ellie would have welcomed a visit from her friend Yenohan — would have enjoyed reading to her in the bedroom, as she used to — but she hadn't seen Yenohan since the policeman burnt down the bark shelters two years before.

****

Yenohan bumped against the unfenced limits of the Mission Station, unable to leave, unable to grow used to this new life, missing the old way with its freedom of travel and variety of food, missing Ellie. Most of the men had gone droving and the women baked damper over open fires and grew lethargic on rations supplied from the store. The only break from the monotony of this life was tending the potatoes.

Mudjingal returned to his family just as the rabbits burrowed in to destroy every potato beneath the ground.

*****

CHAPTER SEVEN

Roger shook his head in disbelief and turned the page of the Sydney Morning Herald, angling the broadsheet to catch the light from the lamp. The sound of spitting sparks punctuated the silence in the room as Nola prodded the fire with a poker. Outside, the wind reminded them it had not yet finished with Winter.

Roger drew on the pipe stem clenched between his teeth. A prolonged sigh escaped his lips, wrapped in a cloud of smoke. From the other side of the fire, Joe stared at the front page, straining to read the print that jumped back and forth with the flickering firelight.

Roger folded the paper and flung it to the floor in disgust. Joe pounced upon it and continued reading as his father rose and leaned on the mantelpiece with both hands, staring into the flames.

'Perhaps it won't last long,' said Nola, rubbing her husband's spine beneath the coarse cotton shirt.

'All this, just because some bloody anarchist shoots an Archduke. Where the hell is Sarajevo, anyway! What the devil has it got to do with us?'

Roger peered below his outstretched arm at his son who was devouring every printed word.

'He'll want to go, you know!'

Joe stopped reading and looked up at his father: 'Wouldn't you?'.

'When I was your age I probably would've.'

Roger left the room and walked onto the verandah to smoke his pipe in peace and thought.

Joe was eighteen. He had listened to the rumours of war for months now and he knew Dan would be enlisting. He wanted to go too. He could see he would have to work on his parents though.

Dan, from the day he turned twenty-one, had succumbed to a wanderlust that periodically steered him towards Sydney. It was as if he were two different men living within one body. While at Grassy Creek, he worked hard, never shirking his responsibilities as cattle and sheep man. Each weekend for the past four years he had ridden over the Pass to court Rebecca Davies. Everyone expected they would marry soon, although Dan never did ask the question.

However, whenever Dan received his share of the profits from the year's clip, he disappeared without a word for weeks at a time. Roger suspected alcohol and the women of Sydney wove a spell upon his younger brother. Dan always returned to Grassy Creek thinner, poorer and chaste, and rode across to Naas Valley to resume his courtship of Rebecca.

Nola followed Roger onto the verandah.

'We may have to face the fact that both Joe and Dan will enlist,' he said, 'and there's no doubt the war'll do Dan good'.

'I'm sure you're right, Roger. But I do think Joe's too young to go.'

But go they did. Joe rode away on Whisper and Dan, along with so many other men from New South Wales, took his own frisky waler. With its wide barrel chest, fine legs, short back and broad head, it could withstand the rigours asked of it on the battlefield.

Ellie buried herself deeper into her books.

*****

Mudjingal didn't return to the droving, but remained with Mooroo and their five children. Each day he went off to ring-bark tall trees, clear scrub, and treat the soil with arsenical insecticides, as ordered by Mr Hockey.

The potatoes and fruit trees had failed. Now they were instructed to plant lucerne. It was hard work, but these lean, wiry Aboriginal men were used to hard work. Again, the crop took and grew tall and healthy with the Summer rains. Again, the rabbits came.

Edgerton was a failure. Three years after being forced to move onto the mission station, Yenohan joined the remaining twenty of her

Wolgal tribe who walked off and returned to their camp on the Murrumbidgee.

And no-one stopped them.

Yenohan's family lived wherever Mudjingal and his sons could find work, mostly along the river. But they returned to Grassy Creek valley in the Summer of 1914 to feast on the jar bon.

*****

Kelvin lit a fire and warmed a large tin of baked beans. He handed me a dishful.

'I feel awful eating all your food.'

'Fran, I know you haven't much food with you. I have plenty and I want to share it. Keep yours till you can get to the shops. Now, I hope that's the end of the matter.'

What could I do but smile and accept?

The day had been beautiful, walking further along Naas Valley, each enjoying our own private space. I couldn't remember feeling so comfortable in another's presence, especially a man's. It felt natural to sit at Kelvin's feet by the evening fire and lean my elbow on his knee. He placed his hand on my neck and my muscles — tight from carrying my pack — eased as his fingers firmly kneeded the knots. Then his hands stopped moving.

'This was a mistake.'

I looked up at him, puzzled.

'What? My following you?'

'Yes.'

I felt angry. I tried to rise; he kept the pressure on my neck.

'Well, hand the keys over and I'll go back. I can leave them on your car.'

I tried to stand again, but the pressure on my neck increased.

'No, Fran. Don't be mad. I just mean that I feel strange, and I don't know what to do about it.'

He pulled me back towards him and rested his chin on my head. I felt the prickle of his stubble move back and forth on my scalp. One of us had to make the first move. I knelt and kissed him.

He cradled me in his arms and we fed the fire with small twigs. Neither of us knew how to make the next move.

'My tent or yours?' I joked.

'I'm old fashioned enough to believe a man should visit a lady's house.'

Kelvin went to my pack and withdrew the tent. He shook it open and handed me the pegs. We erected the tent in silence, then crawled in and made love. Slowly, blissfully. It had been a long time between drinks for both of us, but it didn't show.

I woke before the sun, lying in the crook of Kelvin's arm. He was already awake, watching me. We kissed good morning.

'There's no need to make such an early start today, is there?' I asked.

I knew this was no one-night stand: I'd had a few of those. In the cold light of morning, there is no promise of continuity; this was different. We felt close. The smiles said it all.

'Do you still feel it was a mistake?'

'Yes, I do. But it's something I'll have to deal with.'

We made love again before continuing along Naas Valley.

*****

Ellie saw a thin spiral of smoke rising by the creek. She knew Yenohan's family had been taken to Edgerton Mission Station, which made this reappearance that much more of a surprise. She ran to the camp in search of her friend.

Yenohan's face became full of white, white teeth as she saw Ellie approaching.

They had both changed much in the past three years, as fourteen-year-old girls do. Ellie's hair, once free to tangle as she ran across the paddocks, was now tamed behind her neck with a ribbon, but wisps escaped of their own accord to tickle her cheeks as she ran to her friend. Yenohan's skinny shoulders had curved and were now clothed in white man's clothes. The tight pointed collar was edged with lace, and the box pleats of her navy serge pinafore, caught at the waist by a belt, eased over her young breasts. Her black feet with their pink toenails remained bare.

Ellie linked her arm through Yenohan's elbow and flicked the tight curl hanging over Yenohan's forehead.

'*Mrs Hockey cut all our hair short,*' explained Yenohan.

'*It suits you,*' replied Ellie. She squeezed Yenohan's arm: '*I've missed you Yenohan. Are you back for good?*'

'*I miss you too, Ellie. We don't know what's going on. No one stopped us leaving the mission.*'

Three years' schooling had made a difference to Yenohan's English and they now communicated more freely than they had before.

'*So much has changed since you left,*' bubbled Ellie. '*We now have a school here — say, you could probably come too, Mother is the teacher, and she's really good at it, all the kids love her. Oh yes, and Joe and Dan have gone off to war in France...*'

'*What do you mean?*' asked Yenohan.

'*The Germans are fighting the French and for some reason the English have to be involved.*'

Yenohan had learnt about the world from a globe Mr Hockey kept on his desk, but she couldn't grasp its size, nor how far France was from her home.

'*Will Joe come back?*' asked Yenohan.

'*He'd better!*' replied Ellie. '*Anyway, you're here now, so life won't be near as boring as it has been. Oh Yenohan, I am just so pleased to see you again.*'

Ellie steered Yenohan to her front door, and the two entered the kitchen giggling, as if they had never been apart.

'Look who's turned up,' Ellie said to Nola. Nola walked over to Yenohan and placed her hands on her shoulders, smiling.

'What a young woman you have become, Yenohan!'

Yenohan blushed.

That evening, as Yenohan lay beside her mother in the gunyah, Mooroo rolled on her side and spoke to her daughter in their native tongue.

'I think you should stay here when we go back to the Murrumbidgee. I'm worried the Department will take you again and send you to Cootamundra. You won't be allowed to think or talk Wolgal anymore, and you might end up with a bad family. We know Mr Thompson is one of the good white fellas. Better to clean his house than go where they will beat you. We'll see Mrs Thompson tomorrow. See what she says.'

Mooroo rolled back onto her mat, pleased the dark hid her tears.

The next morning, Yenohan and Mooroo visited Nola and Ellie. It was Yenohan who spoke for them both.

'I know how to do housework from the mission. You reckon I could work here for you?'

Nola saw the pleading look in the eyes of this mother to keep her daughter safe. To refuse would be to risk losing Yenohan to Cootamundra Girls Home: the institution that took young Aboriginal girls and trained them to be servants — and removed every trace of pride in their culture — before farming them out to white employers. Nola also saw the look of anticipation in the eyes of the two young friends.

'Of course she can stay here, so long as that is what you both want. I can put her skills to use, there is no question of that.'

Yenohan returned to her camp for one more night. She sat by the fire till the sky turned pink with the coming sun, singing Wolgal songs with Mooroo and hearing, for the last time, the stories loaded with wisdom on how to live well according to Tribal Law. Then she took her mat, her basket and her possum cloak to the provisions hut where Roger had prepared a corner with a stretcher of saplings and hessian bags for her bed.

*****

As 1914 turned into 1915, Roger rode around his property, a lost soul. He missed his son and his brother and secretly resented being too old to go to war himself. Then he received a letter from his mother:

Dear son,

You know I wouldn't write and ask this if there was any other way, but I am worried about your father. The silly old fool is too damned stubborn to ask for help, but he can't manage on his own any more. With Dan away in France things are going from bad to worse. He is really very ill, but won't even let me call the doctor.

Please, Roger, could you see your way clear to come back home, at least for a while, to help out? But whatever you do, DO NOT TELL HARRY I HAVE ASKED.

Your loving mother.

'I'll have to go,' said Roger, as he handed the letter to Nola.

'Of course you will; we'll all go. The change may do us some good.'

'But what about the school? You've worked so hard to get it established.'

'Most of the children are too old for school now, it's served its purpose. I'll close up until this war has finished. It's just another casualty of countries fighting each other.'

'And Yenohan? What will she do?'

Nola was surprised Roger even asked.

'She'll come too. She's part of our family now and I'm sure she'll be as useful at Melvale as she is here.'

The next day they loaded the dray with everything they would need for the immediate future. Nola took the reins with James beside her and Ellie and Yenohan on the seat behind her, and began the slow journey north to Melvale.

Roger spent the next couple of days rounding up the sheep, aided by two stockmen from the Wolgal tribe, then followed Nola with his flock. The cattle would have to fend for themselves during their absence, but he knew the other Boboyan families would take care of them.

Three days later Nola stopped at the entrance to Melvale for James to open the galvanised pipe gate, then continued down the long dusty drive to pull up before wide concrete steps that led onto the verandah. Nancy rose from the squatters chair and opened her arms in welcome.

'Thank God you're here!'

This was the first time Nola had returned since moving to Boboyan, and the difference in the two homes was even more marked than she had remembered. Family photos occupied every spare shelf, tongue-and-groove walls supported an ornate pressed-metal ceiling. The only things the two dwellings had in common were a scrubbed pine kitchen table and a wood stove, although Nancy's stood in a recess of its own.

Nola followed Nancy into the main bedroom and was shocked to see the head of the Thompson clan grey in hair and skin, and old beyond his years. She bent to kiss his clammy forehead. Despite his fondness for Nola, Harry eyed his daughter-in-law's arrival with suspicion and damaged pride.

'What are you here for lass?' he wheezed.

Nancy threw her hands in the air: 'I've tried to get him to ask you for help, but the stubborn old fool won't listen to me. Reckons he'll be okay after a bit of a rest. He won't even let me fetch the doctor'.

'Don't need a doctor!' Harry's protestation was no more than a whisper.

A week later, Nola heard the barking of the dogs leading the sheep into the paddock out the back of the homestead. She met Roger at the front door. 'Don't get a shock when you see your father. He's failing. He looks awful.'

Roger took one look and immediately hitched his horse to the household sulky and rode into Queanbeyan to fetch the doctor.

The news was not good. Harry's heart was worn out from a lifetime of hard work. Ordered to remain in bed, he folded into the sheets and faced the wall.

There was no question of returning to Grassy Creek. Roger and his family settled in for the duration of the war. Fences needed mending, sheep needed tending, cattle had to be drenched. For the next month they worked from dawn to dusk bringing Melvale back to order. Yenohan, not entirely sure of her position, fitted somewhere between companion and housemaid to Nancy, but this time, she got to sleep inside the house on a bed with springs. Periodically, Roger rode back to Grassy Creek to muster and drench his cattle.

When all the outstanding chores were completed, the women spent most days sitting at the kitchen table stitching their needlework while Roger and the stockmen worked the property, but after a month of inactivity, Nola grew bored and impatient. She was not a lady of leisure. She and Ellie rode the sulky into Queanbeyan and volunteered their services at the hospital.

Daily, they visited the wards: sitting with soldiers who had been sent home early, wounded; reading to those who could no longer see, writing letters for them; bathing remaining limbs; listening to their jokes and tales. They always asked if the boys had come across Joe and Dan. It made the days pass faster for them all. Some of the patients were removed to the isolation ward where they coughed their gassed lungs into spittoons beside their beds.

****

Joe arrived in France during the coldest Winter Europe had known for twenty years. At first, his biggest problem was rain and mud, but the ground soon froze under twenty-five degrees of frost. It would have frozen the very hobs of hell. He spent days marching from billets to trenches along roads that were nothing but shelled-out mud mires. The duckboards only made things worse as pieces, broken from the shelling, speared unwaring soldiers in the calves as they passed.

The trenches were unspeakably disgusting. The abused earth would not hold together. Every time it rained, which it often did for weeks on end, the trenches caved in and buried the soldiers to the waist in slime. The stench was unbearable. Joe could no longer distinguish the smell of mustard gas from rotting bodies.

His spirits lifted enormously when Dan joined his company. They counted themselves lucky. Unlike the men who had been trapped at Gallipoli, they could leave the trenches at the end of each bout of fighting and retreat to relative safety in the chateau where they were billeted, and talk of home.

Leaves fell from trees with the cold, so different from the eucalypts back home; although the glistening white after a fresh fall of snow made Joe's heart ache for Boboyan. Birds departed with the leaves, and the locals said they would return come Spring. At least, they hoped they would. Joe doubted anything would be normal again.

Joe was sitting in a dugout, writing a letter home, when the shell hit. He rushed out to find a hole where Dan had been just minutes before.

Joe's world turned black with rage.

*****

Harry did not recover, and died in the Spring. His had been a tough life, but it had also been a rewarding life and he had made many friends who filled the little church to see him off. With his death, decisions had to be made. Nancy made a pot of tea and ordered Roger and Nola to sit at the table and hear her out.

'I'm tired of battling drought and flood. This is no life for a woman on her own, so I've made provision to surrender Melvale and its stock to you, Roger, and to Dan. I'm sure you'll be able to run things a lot better than I could. I'll move in to Queanbeyan to be with my friends. They've all passed their holdings on to the next generation. It's time life was a bit easier for us.'

Roger kissed her cheek: 'I'm sure I can too, Mum. I won't let you down.'

Nola held Nancy's hand: 'Please stay with us until we return to Boboyan.'

'Of course. Why would I forego the pleasure of having my family fuss over me.'

A week later, Nancy took the telegram from the young lad at her door. Before she opened it, she knew she had lost Dan.

Nola caught a bad cold during 1917, and stayed away from the hospital for fear she might pass her infection on to the patients. She remained in bed for a month while Nancy fussed over her, and the chores around the house fell to Yenohan and Ellie.

The war dragged to an end, and early in 1919, Nancy moved into a modest house in town and Roger brought his family back to Boboyan. He now needed to divide his time between Melvale and Grassy Creek until Joe returned from the war. But something worried Roger: Nola was steadily losing weight, and she coughed into the night with the infection still heavy on her chest. He hoped she hadn't contracted the 'flu that was keeping many of the soldiers in England.

*****

'My tent or yours?' I asked on the third night.

'Same rules apply.'

We laughed and loved again, but come morning it was time to turn around and head back. The trail went on, and we could have too, but Kelvin wanted to be back at Grassy Creek by Friday. We had shared laughter, food, comfort, bed and love.

On the last night on the track, we called in to Horse Gully Hut, but to our disappointment, it was already occupied — by people Kelvin knew. He introduced me to Wilma and Frank, members of the Kosciusko Huts Association.

'This is Fran McMillan. She wanted to see part of the National Trail, so I said she could tag along for a couple of days.'

Wilma eyed me suspiciously, or so it seemed. I felt the guilty pangs of a woman who has been sleeping with a married man.

After tea, we crawled into our separate tents.

Over breakfast Wilma, dressed in shorts — her walking legs firm despite her obvious age — squatted on a rock and asked: 'How's Maggie doing, Kelvin? Haven't seen her for a long time. I suppose she's still involved in tennis?'

'Oh yes. She lives for it. But she's well.'

'That's good. I'm pleased she has an interest. And Trudie?'

'She's kept busy with the kids, always driving them to sport or music. I don't know where she gets her energy from. Must have inherited it from her mother,' they laughed.

'It's nice having grand kids,' said Frank. His large nose, painted with zinc cream, protruded from the brim of a floppy cotton hat. 'You should bring them out walking with you.'

'I plan to, when they're a bit older.'

Wilma Everett hugged Kelvin goodbye: 'Give my love to Maggie. I expect you two to come for dinner when you get back. Right?'

'That would be lovely.'

Kelvin kissed Wilma's sun-wrinkled cheek and shook Frank's hand. Almost as an afterthought, they turned and said goodbye to me.

We parted from the Everetts, who were heading north, and turned towards Grassy Creek. Kelvin seemed quieter than usual on the last leg of our walk. At lunch, I said: 'Meeting the Everetts upset you, didn't it.'

'Fran, I feel wretched. I've never cheated on Maggie before.'

'Do you really consider it cheating?'

He didn't reply.

'Perhaps you should've thought about that before you …'

He put his hand over my mouth and stopped my words mid sentence. His grip was firm, and forced my teeth into my bottom lip. I tasted the sweetness of blood.

'I didn't plan this, Fran! I admit I wondered if you might've had an interest in me. But I did not plan it!'

He removed his hand and turned away. I hurried after him, pulling his arm to stop him.

'I know you didn't plan it, Kelvin. Neither did I. But it's been very special for me, and I don't want to let it go.'

He turned to face me. 'Neither do I.'

We finished the few kilometres of our journey in silence, each deep within our own thoughts. When we reached our vehicles, Kelvin enquired about my plans for the weekend.

'We could still do with a hand, if you're interested.'

'Wouldn't it be awkward, us working together with your friends looking on?'

'They won't know. It won't be any different from last weekend.'

'No, but we will, and I don't know that I'm a good enough actor to pretend nothing's happened.'

'Well, see how you feel in the morning.'

We each erected our own tent — to fool Norman and the gang when they arrived the next day — but spent the night together. There was sadness in my tent the next morning as Kelvin unwound his body from mine.

'Is that the last time we'll make love?' I asked.

Kelvin turned to me as he buttoned his flanny. The pain in his eyes spoke volumes.

Sitting by the fire, waiting for the rest of the work party to arrive, I made the decision to stay on for the weekend. It was more an act of procrastination than a conscious decision to work on the Thompson's homestead. Geehi would have to wait for another visit.

Norman, Geoff and Mike arrived in convoy, and they were genuinely pleased to find me still camped at the hut. Norman threw me a two-kilo packet of organically grown, unbleached self-raising flour.

'Here girlie, thought you might still be around. We'll get the fire going soon as we open up and you can cook us one of your super-duper dampers.'

He gave me a welcome hug.

A dark-haired young woman unfurled her long body from the passenger seat of Geoff's small sedan and removed her sunglasses.

'I suppose you're Fran. Geoff said you might be here. I'm Gloria.'

Gloria gathered her long thick hair into a band at the nape of her neck and threw me a spade from the boot. I took to her immediately.

'How are you at gardening?' She asked me.

'My plants usually die, but I'm great on the end of a pick.'

'Good. Let's bash this front garden into shape, then.'

Kelvin smiled and went into the building to get the fire going for the damper.

It seemed I had known these people for years, not simply for one week. I am a loner by nature. We were all loners, working together for a common cause.

I was pleased to find that the presence of Geoff's fiancé did not inhibit his enthusiasm for story telling. As we savoured the morning-tea damper, Gloria laughed along with the rest of us, occasionally correcting a detail or adding her point of view as Geoff recounted their week-long walk from Lake St. Clair to Cradle Mountain in the highlands of Tasmania one mid-Winter.

'Most people do it from the other direction because it's downhill. But we l-l-like a challenge.'

We rinsed our mugs and Gloria and I returned to a tangle of weeds choking red geraniums either side of the front steps. Norman wriggled his way underneath the building with a torch to check on the foundations. His feet dangled from the rocks, like enormous skink tails.

Mike, satisfied that his windows would now keep the snow on the outside of the building, scrambled up the ladder to repair the flashing where the roof met the verandah.

*****

Ellie's zest for life returned with her to Grassy Creek. When not occupied with tending the homestead or her mother, she rode the high plains with Yenohan, reacquainting herself with the mountain trees she loved, waiting for Joe to return from France.

Even Nola responded well to the return to the dryness of the high country. Ellie wrapped a blanket around Nola's shoulders and they sat in the sun on the front verandah, out of the breeze. They were there when Joe, wearing his uniform, rode up on Whisper.

The Joe who returned from war was not the Joe who had left Boboyan four years ago. Ellie almost did not recognise him, he had changed so much: his red hair had turned a deep auburn, as was the beard he now wore, and his once-youthful shoulders carried the bulk of manhood. He refused to discuss his time in France, even with Ellie.

A couple of weeks after his return, when Ellie and Yenohan were digging potatoes from the patch, Joe came to help. 'I'm moving up to the Mount Clear hut tomorrow, Ellie.'

She sat back on her heels, faced smeared with dirt, wondering if the sorrow that had fallen on her family would ever lift. Having Joe back was the only brightness in her days.

'It's James,' Joe continued. 'Having him around with his black curls and cheeky grin — I can't help it, he just is so like Dan. I need time to get used to the fact that Dan's not around any more. I hope you understand.'

As Ellie looked at Yenohan, she noticed her brown eyes were brimming with tears as well.

*****

CHAPTER EIGHT

Norman said: 'The foundations are sound. I'd say we're on target for the opening'. Kelvin balanced on the saw horse behind me and handed me a sandwich. I accepted it, wondering if Norman's inquisitive eyes had worked out our secret. The sky had that whiteness that comes with cold. Since the previous weekend, the temperature had not risen above ten degrees celsius. Winter was all but here.

'When's the opening?' I asked; not that I would be able to take part, I would be back in Queensland by then.

'We're aiming for Spring, probably mid October,' replied Norman. 'It'll be a terrific day. They always are. Everyone who has ties with the building turns up. It'd be nice if you could make it too, Fran.'

'I doubt I could make two trips in one year, tempting though it is.'

'You've gotta have lace curtains!' We all looked at Mike in surprise.

'Lace curtains?' Asked Gloria.

'My Nan has lace curtains, and this house looks like hers,' replied Mike.

'Then it shall have lace curtains,' agreed Norman.

'I'll get Nan to make them then, eh?'

Everyone nodded in agreement. Norman delegated the afternoon's jobs.

Gloria and I collected shovels and buckets from a little storeroom off the end of the verandah and began removing years of ash from the living room fireplace. Our nostrils soon became clogged and our faces grew blacker with each bucketful of ash we carried outside, until we resembled chimney sweeps of old. We cheered when our spades finally scraped the long-buried concrete hearth.

Already so dirty, we filled our buckets with clay and made a thick slurry to poke between the rocks in the chimneys. Gloria wiped a black finger down my nose, then continued to paint my face with sticky mud. Our laughter brought everyone outside to watch the face painting that followed.

We lit a fire in the fresh fireplace, boiled the billy, and cleaned our faces and our arms. Cooking smells and camaraderie filled the living room as night wrapped around the hut. With the tools neatly stored on the verandah, it regained its homely atmosphere. I balanced on my camp stool and Kelvin rested against my knees. I thought about how familiar his actions must appear to all in the room, but it wasn't my place to correct this familiarity.

The evening was a repeat of the previous Saturday night: wine; crinkling chip packets; storytelling; laughter. As I curled into my sleeping bag sometime after midnight, the heat from my body released the smell of our love-making of the morning.

I awoke to a white world again. Kelvin was returning to his ute after his morning walk and came to my tent where I knelt, bleary-eyed, at the entrance.

'Did you sleep okay?' He asked.

'Not too bad, but I was hoping for a visit through the night.'

'It seemed to me that we'd said goodbye yesterday morning. I thought it best not to prolong the agony. And it is an agony, Fran.'

'You're probably right, Kelvin. I've always been the selfish sort.'

He held his hand out to give me a hoist up, and kept hold as we approached the hut, dropping my hand to push the door open. The gang had already finished breakfast and Norman was allocating the most pressing jobs for the day.

'Looks as if Winter's here early, so this'll have to be our last weekend before next Spring. We can't do much with it snowing all the time. There's no use continuing with the garden, Gloria, so you and Geoff can replace the iron on the hearth, then scrub the soot off the wall above the fireplace. God knows how it got there. Kelvin, what say you and Fran finish the reflooring in the main bedroom? Mike and I'll shin up onto the roof and give it a final once over.'

He clapped his hands as we huddled, motionless, by the fire. 'Come on! Get moving! Choppy choppy!'

We all groaned to our feet; it was very cold.

In the bedroom, Kelvin began laying new boards on the bearers, ready for nailing. Even though I had been working in this room for a few days, I hadn't looked up at the ceiling until now. I was disappointed to see most of the ceiling boards were missing. I had thought the work on the hut was just about finished.

'I suppose they've all got to be replaced before open day!'

Kelvin stopped positioning the floorboards to look where I was pointing.

'Oh no! Not them! That's history!'

'How do you mean?'

'The woman who lived here, her name was Nola as I recall, died during a flood. She had TB. They couldn't get her over the Murrumbidgee to Cooma, so they had to bury her here. They used the ceiling boards to make her coffin.'

'Oh Kelvin, that's awful. The poor woman!'

Kelvin sat back on his heels: 'It's the family I feel sorry for. She was out of it, so she wouldn't have known the trial it must have been for her hubby and kids. You can see the grave just over the rise behind the house if you feel like a walk.'

At lunchtime I pulled on my coat and walked to the grave. It was a sad sight. An ornate wrought iron fence, erected to keep cattle out, lay on the ground in a tangle of hawthorn bushes. The ground was rutted by pigs. Pink and white periwinkle blossoms peeped through the snow.

A hand-carved wooden cross stood askew at the head of the grave, and into it were burned the words:

Nola Thompson

wife of Roger

mother of Joseph, Eleanor, James

R.I.P.

26 July 1919

I felt an overwhelming sadness for this woman whom I had never known, but whose house I had shared. I returned to the hut, determined to do all I could to restore her home in the few remaining hours.

*****

Sheets of water ran down the window pane, distorting the multi-coloured tree trunk beyond Nola's bedroom. Ellie turned away from the flooding world and brushed a splinter of wood from her mother's cheek, expecting the pale lips to curve into a smile of gratitude. More splinters and grit floated down and flecked Nola's dress as Joe jemmied the boards from the ceiling. Ellie pulled the blanket up over her mother, but stopped short of covering her gaunt freckled face, now peaceful.

On the rise beyond the homestead, rain poured from Roger's hair to mix with mud as it splashed onto his face. Through rain, slush, snow and tears he worked. Each time the pick plunged into the cold hard earth, it bounced off rock, jarring his arms. He returned to their home to help Joe put the finishing touches to the pitiful box, then wrapped the blanket around his wife and gently lowered her into it. Rope, bound around the casket, served as handles. Roger, Ellie, Joe and James lifted their wife and mother and walked through the teeming rain to the grave awaiting her.

Yenohan watched the procession from the door of the provisions hut with inexpressible grief. Nola's passing only heightened her own loneliness. She did not belong with this family whose various sorrows hung heavily on the air, she belonged with her own people, and with her own mother whom she had not seen since she had begged the Thompsons to take and protect her. She had, however, heard from the Wolgal stockmen who worked in these mountains that Mudjingal had headed for Brungle Mission Station, 100 miles across the high mountains.

Yenohan neatly folded the clothes Nola and Ellie had made for her and left them on her stretcher and then, without knowing how she would find her family, walked out into the pouring rain .When Ellie returned, she saw that Yenohan had vanished.

*****

The farewells were easier second time around, and the work party all reckoned I'd be back for the open day. I wasn't so sure. Kelvin gently pulled my elbow and held me as the other vehicles left the circle of pines. We kissed and hugged, not wanting to let go.

'What should we do?' I couldn't help it, my eyes were watering.

'I can't see there's much we can do, Fran. But for the record, it has been very special for me too.'

Then he grinned. 'Even if you are young enough to be my daughter.'

'Only just. You'd have been very precocious to have fathered me.'

He rested his chin on my head; the stubble had softened over the week.

'Let's keep in touch, just in case.'

We exchanged e-mail addresses: his at work and mine at home.

I drove back through Namadgi National Park, but the landscape that had so enchanted me three weeks before flew past my window unnoticed. I drove through the forest, descended steep Fitz's Hill, passed Mount Tennent and crossed the old wooden bridge over the Murrumbidgee at Tharwa, all in a daze, following the dusty tail-lights of the Landcruiser. Then we merged with traffic on the Monaro Highway and I lost sight of them.

Traffic swirled around my car like a river in a hurry to cross the Monaro Plains, heading towards Canberra. The smell of car fumes, the bustle of people rushing in and out of the shopping mall at Tuggeranong, the noise, row upon row of solid brick houses, all crowded in on me. I wished I could turn the clock back and join the Thompsons in their homestead.

*****

Yenohan had never been to these mountains before. Her family had always gone towards the sea when Winter came. After leaving Grassy Creek, she sought out Pullerkuinergong, who was mustering cattle on Boboyan Hill, to ask the way over the mountains. He knew this area well; had ridden it many times.

He pointed to the mountain in the west: 'Go around that mountain, then cross up to the plains through the gap. The cattlemen won't be there now because of the snow. Cross to the other side, find the Goobarragandra River and follow it all the way down till it meets the Tumut River. It will lead straight to Brungle.'

She climbed high enough for the rain to stop and the snow to fall. Four years of living with white people had not taken away her knowledge of bush food. She had a full belly when she crawled beneath an overhanging rock and slept till morning, warm in her possum cloak. Seven days later, weary and footsore, she reached Mooroo.

*****

Throughout history, the kitchen table has served as the centrepiece of the home. The heart of the home. I sat at the kitchen table of my friend and fellow woodworker, Jill, not far from the Canberra suburb of Chapman, where Kelvin lived. She and I had been friends since we left high school, and I always stayed with her when I was in Canberra for the National Folk Festival.

If it were possible for an inanimate object to blush, Jill's kitchen table would have turned from gold to deep scarlet many a time over the years as, often late into the night, we laughed and cried our way through our deepest secrets. This night I told her of my fling with Kelvin. She told me of a long distance affair she was having via the internet.

For the next four days, we camped in the grounds of the Folk Festival, lost in a surreal world of music, dance and friendship: the annual gathering of our own tribes, devoid of class, state or national boundaries.

I danced until my feet screamed for a break, then I sang until my voice gave way. With my head in a fuzz, I crawled into my tent in the early hours of each morning, resenting my body's demands for rest in order to do it all again.

As we discussed and sang of the sad state of the world post 9/11, seeking solutions through the haze of Guinness and optimism, Kelvin seemed far away — not only a few kilometres.

During the following days, I accepted the fact that, despite our very genuine feelings for each other, our worlds were too disparate for there ever to be a future for us.

The festival drew to a close and we dispersed to the four corners of the globe for another twelve months. I farewelled Jill and her kitchen table and made the slow trip back to Queensland.

It was slow of necessity. I needed to replenish my stock of timber and I knew of a few small sawmills where old millers kept special pieces aside in their back sheds. They produced stunning lengths of timber for me to admire, and invariably said they had been saving them for some special purpose for themselves — but could be persuaded to hand them over, for a price.

I dipped into the bank account I maintained solely for this purpose: the remnants of my father's meagre estate.

*****

Wet clothes festooned bushes on the banks of Brungle River. Yenohan and Mooroo chatted with other women as they stirred white clothes bubbling in a copper over a fire and watched children at play in the river: swinging from ropes; dive-bombing; skimming stones; white smiles flashing amidst sparkling water.

As the dew began to gather, Yenohan and Mooroo folded the dry laundry into a cane pram and wheeled it back to their house on the hill, well away from the station manager's house and ration store. The bunyip kept her brothers safe by inhabiting the river of an evening. No child dared go near it then.

As white graziers had gradually moved in to the Murrumbidgee River valley, the land over which the Wolgal people were able to range and hunt had become smaller and smaller. Mudjingal was left with little choice but to move his family to Brungle Mission Station near Tumut. He was one of the last of his tribe to do so. There he built a three-roomed hut using stringybark for the framework and tin, foraged from the Tumut dump, for the walls and roof. They dug up white clay, mixed it to a slurry with water, and whitewashed the internal hessian walls with brushes made from tussock grass. Brungle Mission Station, beside Brungle River in a grassy basin ringed by hills and mountains, was a vast improvement on Edgerton Mission Station. Twenty families already lived there. It had the atmosphere of "home".

The Aboriginal people caught fish in the river and speared rabbits in the hills — revenge of sorts for the destruction these pests had caused at Edgerton — and there was little doubt that the children were more content at Brungle. Mudjingal passed on to his sons his skill of bending wire into a hook to remove witchetty grubs from trunks of the eucalyptus trees. Vegetable gardens and orchards bore fruit.

In the Spring, after a week spent docking lambs' tails on a nearby sheep station, Mudjingal arrived home with a sackful of delicacies that he threw on the fire to burn off the wool. Sometimes he would return with a dead sheep over his saddle and hang it overnight to drain and set in a tree by their house.

Yenohan learnt how to clean the tripe bag ready for steaming. Mooroo cooked the sheep's head and pressed the brawn hard under rocks. Yenohan and her brothers stretched and cleaned the fleece which, when it was dry and sweet, Mudjingal sewed into a bag and stuffed with straw: so cosy in the nights when buckets of water, left out overnight, turned to ice.

But no matter how spotless Mooroo kept her home and her children, or how well fed and neatly dressed, she lived in fear of the white fellas who periodically patrolled the station looking to rescue "neglected children" from their parents.

Yenohan was now too old to attend school on Brungle Station, and she lay awake at night fearful that she might yet be sent to Cootamundra Girls Home. Last month her friend, Ninim, had come back to Brungle after escaping from her white boss who had selected her from Cootamundra the year before. The station manager allowed Ninim to remain with her family long enough for her bruises to fade to yellow, then sent her back to Cootamundra to receive her punishment for running away.

One night, Mooroo crept in to lie beside Yenohan on her sleeping mat, much as she had done once before: 'Yenohan, you must go back to the Thompsons before a bad whiteman takes you. You'll be safe there. Leave before Mudjingal wakes. Take his pack horse.'

Yenohan clung to Mooroo until the morning sky began to lighten, then tiptoed out of her home and rode back over the mountains to Grassy Creek.

Ellie, who had grown used to Yenohan's disappearances and reappearances, cleared out the corner of the provisions hut, pleased to have her friend return; pleased to accept Yenohan's help cooking for the extra men who had arrived at Grassy Creek for summer work.

****

PART TWO

...

CHAPTER NINE

*E*llie tapped the leg of her moleskin trousers with her stock-whip as she closed the front door to Grassy Creek and stepped down from the verandah.

She looked to the westward sky to make sure it was still clear. High fine clouds wisped across from the north-east with the promise of good weather. There was a hint of Spring in the air, despite the bracing chill of an early-morning breeze. Only last week, the Pallid Cuckoo had announced its arrival with a persistent staccato 'pip-pip-pip-pip', and had kept it up day and night. It would soon find a mate.

Ellie tightened the girth strap under Freckles and swung onto the saddle, then leaned over and unlooped the reins of her packhorse from the railing.

'Reckon we're as ready as we'll ever be,' she said. Freckles flicked his ears backwards, heeding his mistress's voice. Balancing *her stock-whip on the shoulder of her sturdy cotton shirt, she headed across Pheasant Pass towards Nan's homestead.*

****

The Big Men of the wool industry dominated the leases on the snow belt leaving small pastoralists, such as the Thompsons, the choice of either grazing illegally on crown land or subleasing from wealthy graziers. Ellie saw there would be advantages in the pastoralists of Boboyan district working together, and so she had suggested, during a social gathering at the Robinsons, that the local families take up individual leases, then join forces and drive their collective herd westward over Bimberi Range, through Murray's Gap onto the plains of Currango, thus spelling their own valleys and hills for recovery over Summer.

They hadn't needed much convincing, as continual grazing and the very dry years of the early '20s had taken their toll on the wiry tussock grass upon which they depended. Roger was more than happy to let his daughter make these decisions. She had matured into an intelligent, sensible woman. So like Nola.

These days, he mostly stayed up north at Melvale; it was easier than being at Grassy Creek where, each evening as he lay down to sleep, he looked at the missing ceiling and mourned his wife afresh. He decided he should move permanently to Melvale after this drive. He was now fifty-one years of age and the physically demanding life he had led prematurely robbed him of energy and stamina. He no longer had the agility that had seen him through the rough alpine Winter of 1910.

Grassy Creek homestead had blossomed under Ellie Thompson's care. Now a spacious five-roomed dwelling, it floated on a sea of flowers that filled the house yard, separated from the rest of the Thompson land by a whitewashed picket fence. There were gooseberries all around, and cherry trees, all coaxed to life during dry months by judicious use of household waste water.

Ellie maintained a flock of a hundred turkeys that she drove from valley to valley seeking out the best pasture. Periodically, she selected some to butcher and sell to other pastoralists who welcomed the change from the monotonous diet of bully beef and mutton.

The outside world was creeping into Boboyan: John Davies brought the first motorised truck to the valley, resupplying provisions would now be much easier for him. A turban-wrapped Indian hawker always called on Ellie when he passed through the district with his wagon dripping with pots and pans, brooms and dusters. She bought materials from him — muslin, flannelette, serge — and made clothes for the family on a treadle machine Joe had bought in Sydney with the profits of last year's cattle sales.

The year before, he had returned with an upright piano strapped to the dray. Ellie hardly noticed its less than perfect pitch as her fingers floated over the keys, finding familiar tunes.

At Ellie's request, one end of the verandah was enclosed to make a room for her to sew, read, write, gaze out over Grassy Creek, and keep her daily diary and the family's accounts.

Now that Joe had moved to the Mount Clear hut and James preferred to sleep in the old hut amongst the pines, Ellie had the lean-to bedroom to herself.

A new kitchen was built where the back door used to be, right next to her bedroom. It had a fireplace of its own and a wood fuel stove. How Nola would have treasured such a possession. A tapered chimney, identical to the one in the living room, took the smoke skywards.

Upon Ellie's insistence the family, appropriately dressed, gathered at Grassy Creek each Sunday for lunch. The food was much the same as any other day of the week: roast mutton with vegetables picked that morning from their garden, but on Sundays the table was dressed with a linen cloth and napkins — each contained by a tooled leather ring — fine china, silver cutlery and a crystal cruet set.

In all seasons except Winter, a bowl of flowers squatted in the centre of the table. Slowly but surely, refinement had come to Grassy Creek.

Yenohan, now a handsome woman of twenty-four, also graced the dining table and shared the Summer days with the Thompson family, as a companion to Ellie and as a help around the homestead.

She continued to wear her hair cut short, and had the habit of flicking the curls out of her eyes as she ate her meal. Her infectious laughter filled the house. She wore a blue gabardine skirt and white cotton blouses, sewn by Ellie, over undergarments Mooroo had fashioned from laundered calico flour bags. Her full mauve lips and soft rounded nose attested to her Aboriginal ancestry. She told Ellie that, now she was a woman, she was free to be with her own family without fear of being sent to Cootamundra, and so each year, as Winter approached, she left her Grassy Creek clothes neatly folded on the stretcher in the provisions hut and rode off. Ellie had no reason to doubt Yenohan crossed the mountains to her family at Brungle Mission Station.

James, at fifteen, had matured beyond his years. He shared the old hut with Alec's ghost, much as Joe did with Dan's ghost in the Mount Clear hut. Joe's nightmares gradually slowed as wartime memories receded, and he and James grew closer.

The Thompson cattle and sheep grazed a long way from the homestead these days. Joe and James had spent the past two weeks mustering cattle along Horse Gully — camping in the mud hut on the banks of Naas Creek, sharing their tucker, their stories and their fire, as brothers do.

Once the mustering was completed, Joe and James drove their cattle through Smoker's Yards at the foot of Sentry Box Mountain and on to Yaouk Homestead to rendezvous with Stan Robinson and

John Davies. Altogether they had a large mob nearing a thousand head ready for the drive up onto Currango Plains further west.

*****

By the time I settled back into my two-bedroom worker's cottage in Paddington, Autumn was nudging the Summer heat out of Brisbane. I hadn't noticed how closely the Thompson homestead in Namadgi National Park resembled my own home. I unloaded the timber into my workshop beneath the house, and stickered it for drying. It would be a couple of years before it would be stable enough to convert to furniture.

Each pile of timber in my workshop represented a year's purchase. I unstacked the oldest pile from 1998 and sorted through the red cedar I had brought back from Atherton Tableland in far north Queensland. The irony that I had bought it in the year of my divorce was not lost on me: in many ways, I felt I was starting out on a new life. It probably wouldn't be with Kelvin — he carried too much baggage — but I had turned an emotional corner during my southern trip.

I rested my nose on the rough plank and breathed its spicy aroma. It smelt like Mike's sash windows. I had a special project in mind for this timber. When I had acquired the deep red coloured cedar, I had made a promise to myself that I would make something for my own home, not for some furniture to sell at the Saturday markets.

I spent the next few days designing a dining room chair, using the skills I had learnt at TAFE a few years earlier. I had enough timber to make six chairs: slender backs arched sufficiently to fill the small of the back; large comfortable seats to fit the spreading hips of middle-aged friends who would occupy them during intimate hours after dinner parties, trying new bottles of wine.

On a large sheet of graph paper I drew intricate Celtic knots that would grow on a canvas, stitch by stitch, and be ready to upholster the seats when I had finished making the chairs.

For the next six months, between making multiple natural-edged coffee tables for the markets, I worked on my dining chairs. The table would have to wait until next year.

Kelvin and I sent sporadic e-mails, but we were unsure what to say to each other.

*****

Roger and his Wolgal stockmen set out from Melvale with six hundred wethers at the same time as Joe and James left Grassy Creek with the cattle. The newly-shorn animals sprang with lightness into their journey.

At first they followed the usual route south to Boboyan, stopping each evening to rest men and sheep — the first night at Tuggeranong, the second at Tharwa — but when they reached Naas Reserve, they veered off the southern track and followed Gudgenby River westward, urging the flock up gruelling Fitz's Hill.

They crossed over into Orroral Valley, and Roger steered his flock around the reserve to the rear of Orroral Homestead. He penned his sheep in yards overnight to share the grass with grey kangaroos who peered disdainfully down their long noses at the woolly beasts.

Roger accepted the hospitality offered by the owner of Orroral Homestead. His two stockmen camped out in the yard, close to the sheep. Mornings began early at Orroral. At four o'clock, Roger was awakened by movement in the kitchen and the smell of freshly cooked damper.

Orroral Valley glowed golden with the coming sun as they released the sheep from the yard and headed towards Fishloch Yards. Here they rested for an hour before scrambling up the high barren range to Cotter's Gap. Through the gap, they needed to restrain the sheep from breaking away as they took the fall down into the Cotter Valley and crossed Pond Creek.

Roger and his stockmen reached deserted Cotter Homestead on the fifth day after they set out from Melvale. They busied themselves making hurdles from local scrub so the sheep could graze safely while they awaited the arrival of the mob from Boboyan with the cattle.

*****

Ellie and Nan had remained behind to close down the houses for the month it would take to settle the stock onto Currango Plains, then return. The women's packhorses had a full load for the trip. Each carried a dozen loaves of bread, a cooked leg of lamb, tins of jam, flour, tea and vegetables — they would shoot roos and rabbits on the way — and a plum pudding Nan thought would lift their spirits at the end of the long journey.

The sun was sliding behind Sentry Box Mountain when Ellie and Nan saw a horseman riding towards them. Ellie knew by the set of the rider that it was Joe on Whisper. He turned his horse's head and fell in beside the two women. Ellie smiled at her brother.

They rode on to Yaouk and joined the other drovers resting around the fire. Nan greeted her husband, John, and her son, Steven. Rebecca had departed from the family home not long after the finish of the war. Unable to come to grips with Dan's death, she apprenticed herself to a tailor in Sydney. Nan hoped her daughter would find what she was looking for there.

'How's your day been, Ellie?'

The question came from Walter Robinson, the twenty-four-year-old son of Stan.

Ellie sank cross-legged to the ground: 'Oh, pretty uneventful Walter. Ask me the same question tomorrow night and I might have a different answer!'

Ellie had known Walter most of her life. He had been away droving in Queensland for the past five years and had matured from the gangly youth she remembered into a tall thin man with a prominent Adam's apple.

The trip onto Currango Plains didn't require the thirteen people who had gathered at Yaouk Homestead for the journey, but not one of them would miss this new adventure.

Jack Swift had accepted the position of camp cook. He had never taken another woman since his wife, Annie, had died giving birth to Michael; and Michael had not come home from the war. Now completely alone, Jack no longer ran stock on his property, but drifted around helping out wherever he could.

Ellie hadn't realised how tired she felt until Jack nudged her foot, jarring her out of a sleep. He handed her a dish of stew with dumplings floating on top.

'Here, get this into you.'

Suppressing the urge to drift back to sleep, she thanked the cook and ate heartily. She hadn't realised how hungry she was, either.

The Aboriginal stockmen, preferring to sleep away from the white fellas' camp, took turns riding around the cattle through the night, and sleeping with one eye open for wild dogs that patrolled beyond the glow of the fire.

The next Ellie knew was the clang of a spoon on the side of the porridge pot, announcing breakfast. Every shivering bone in her body ached from the previous day's ride and the hard earth that had been her bed.

The working black and white dogs circled impatiently, waiting for the humans to eat their oats and pack their saddlebags. As soon as the drovers mounted their horses, the dogs lay flat on their bellies, ears pointed, waiting for their orders. James, astride his chestnut mare, pushed his hat firmly onto his springy black curls and tightened the chin strap. He placed two fingers between his teeth and whistled the instructions that sent the dogs darting around the cattle, turning their heads north.

High wispy clouds in the eastern sky drew colour from the sun as the procession ambled off. It was hard going, although the steep slopes through which they passed did help contain the cattle that were constantly trying to break away.

Under the Pastures Protection Act, a legislation designed to ensure drovers didn't tarry on the lush grasses en route, they were obliged to travel a minimum of six miles each day until they reached the plains. The men had just managed their required distance on the first two days and Ellie knew they would be travelling short once they reached the unforgiving Bimberi Range. They camped the night beside Old Yaouk Creek, ready for the climb the next day.

During the scramble through Yaouk Gap Ellie noticed Walter was riding with her and Nan. That night, as they rested their exhausted bodies by the fire, he barely left her side, attentive to her every need. When she withdrew to relieve herself behind a tree, Joe followed and waited beyond the fire's light until she had completed her task.

'Is Walter bothering you?' He asked.

'He's been following me everywhere I go like a pesky blowfly, but he's harmless enough. He seems to have taken a fancy to me — for God's sake, after all this time! He's like another brother.'

'Well, you let me know if you want me to have a word with him.'

'Thanks Joe, but I'll be able to take care of him.'

'I'm sure you will!' he said with a grin.

As they returned to the fire, Walter was peering intently in their direction through bushy eyebrows. Ellie sat next to him and made light conversation. Walter unknitted his eyebrows and blushed. His Adam's apple bobbed as he swallowed fresh air.

*****

The Boboyan cattle met up with Roger's sheep at Cotter Homestead. The next morning, they scrabbled their way up the steep, shaley Bimberi Range through Murray's Gap, a thousand cattle up front, six hundred wethers behind, and in so doing, crossed from the Federal Capital Territory into New South Wales. They rested the animals and ate their lunch on top of the world then, on the final stage of their journey, took the fall down onto Currango Plains.

These Boboyan folk, used to frost hollows and mountain ranges, were unprepared for the enormous sea of golden grass that flowed westward, to vanish behind distant mountains. To the south-west, the plains were bordered by wave upon wave of snow gum ridges fading into the distance. To the east, Bimberi Peak and Mount Murray lay like huge bosoms in the Brindabella Range.

They felt they had discovered a new land. They were, therefore, surprised to find a new homestead of solid slabs, crowned by a shining iron roof, nestled in a spectacular site at the top of a clearing. Its three panelled doors opened onto a wide split *slab verandah with bench seats lining the wall.*

Beyond the homestead sprawled stockyards with three tiers of solid planks checked into hefty uprights. Cherry and apple trees and gooseberries were heavy with the promise of fruit. Old mother Bimberi knelt in the early evening shadows with the last of the sun's rays touching her head as a man, well past middle age, waddled out to greet them.

'Youse the Boboyan mob?'

His legs were bowed as if his horse had just galloped out from between them and his whiskers tangled around the buttons on his shirt.

'News travels fast,' replied Joe. He dismounted and shook the fellow's hand.

'Jim Elemore's the name. Youse can pen the sheep in them yards if you like, then come in and have a cuppa. We seen you coming, and the missus's got the kettle on.'

The men secured the sheep then gathered on the verandah, not wanting to crowd the house. Jim Elemore stood with his back against the verandah rail and leaned on one elbow. He screwed his face into a question: 'Why'd you come up the Bimberi?'

'This is our first time up here, and we needed to meet somewhere central. You see, I've come from Queanbeyan and the rest of the mob have come from Boboyan,' replied Roger.

'But all the same, youse are better off meeting up on the plains. You Boboyan mob should've come up the 'Bidgee!'

'Local knowledge, eh? Thanks Jim. We'll know better next time.'

The house was oriented to the east, partly for the views, but mostly to welcome the summer coolness that came from the east. The heat from the west was taken care of by a thick stand of black sallees.

Ellie and Nan pulled off their elastic-sided boots and entered the homestead. A multiple-chinned woman was pouring hot water into an enormous teapot with one hand and directing her four excitable children with the other. She shook Ellie's hand, then Nan's, as she continued to pour.

'G'day my dears. I'm Bessie. Would you mind closing the screen door? The blowies'll end up driving us mad otherwise. These are me kids: Mary, Bertie, Liz and Edward.'

She nodded at the smiling faces on the four bodies squirming expectantly by the kitchen table. Bessie wrapped a cloth around two practised hands and opened the oven door. She withdrew a very large tray of golden scones. The kids oohed their appreciation as she transferred the scones to a plate and handed it to Ellie.

'Here love, take these out to the men, will you?'

Bessie swayed after Ellie with the pot of tea and Nan carried the butter crock and a huge jar of raspberry jam, dodging the four bodies following the scones.

Everyone thanked the Elemores through stuffed mouths. Bessie waved away their compliments as if shooing a blowie. Jim Elemore stroked his ample beard and turned to discuss the business of the day with the men. He warned them to dodge the damp reedy hollows that were infested with small snails.

'When me sheep get into them soaks, some of them die and go black. I spread bluestone round. That seems to fix them. I suggest you do the same.'

After dinner Jim produced bottles of spirit of dubious origin and started into politics: 'I'm blowed if I can see why Australian Estates, who own Currango Homestead I'll have you know, should have control of 90,000 acres of grazing land up here. Me and some mates are trying to stop them rich graziers taking all the land on the snow belt.' He winked, 'and we've got the ear of the Labor Party'.

'We didn't expect to find anyone settled up here,' said Roger. 'This house looks new.'

'*Well, we couldn't see why them big buggers should have it all their own way, so we got a lease and built here. Just let them try to move us now!*'

The discussion went on well into the night, but by then Ellie and Nan had retired to the end room to sleep in comfort. The men would camp outside with the stock.

Ellie plumped up the feather pillow and leant it against the narrow iron bedstead and angled her book towards the yellow glow from the kerosene lamp. As she turned the pages, she heard Nan's steady breathing in the twin bed across the room.

She looked at the back of Nan's head with its neatly-cut grey hair spread on the pillow. Ellie didn't need a mother-figure very often, she had grown fiercely independent since Nola's death five years before, but she knew Nan was there for her should the need arise. Perhaps more aunt than mother. Ellie would never admit that Nan was her role model, but the older woman anticipated the younger woman's every move as though she laid the path open for her.

Nan sensed Ellie's watching and rolled over, leaning her head on her wrist.

'*This's a very ambitious plan of yours, Ellie.*'

'*It's not only me. We're all playing a part.*'

'*Yes, but it was your idea in the first place. Don't get me wrong, I reckon it's got merit, but none of our men would have had the courage to suggest it. They're too stuck in their ways.*'

Ellie marked her page and closed the book.

'It doesn't take courage Nan, just forward thinking. We expect too much from our land. It will be all the better for the spell.'

'Well, I can't argue with you there.'

Nan yawned and stretched.

'Don't read too long, will you dear. Big day tomorrow. We'll finally see what this promised land holds for us.'

Ellie said goodnight, and cupped her hand around the top of the glass chimney and blew out the lamp. The smell of warm kerosene lingered in the room.

Nan's breathing slowed into the steady rhythm of sleep and blended with the hooting of owls and the clinking of horses' hobbles through the open window. Ellie lay cradling her head in her interlaced fingers, watching the shadows of the trees dance on the tar-papered walls. She knew this was all her idea, and was proud of it. Her plans were much more ambitious than Roger's had ever been. Until this year, the Thompson stock had moved between Melvale and Grassy Creek on a yearly basis to fatten in the grassy valleys. At no stage had Roger contemplated moving further afield — not until Ellie had taken charge of the decision-making. Although Joe was older, she had assumed the role of running the family properties, it came naturally to her. Joe's talents were on horseback. He rarely left the saddle, except to sleep, and then it often supported his head. The sheep and cattle remained firmly under Joe's control, the homestead and the accounts under hers. But she could see that, with careful management, the Boboyan stock had the potential to be the envy of the snow belt. Their sheep, forced to search for feed during the dry years, were producing fine wool that was sought after in Sydney. She had listened with interest to the stockmen who passed through the valley, camping the night in the old hut; listened to their ideas, and kept the best for herself. Only a few hours of darkness remained when Ellie finally switched off her mind.

With morning, they rode into a thick fog; formed as cold air from the Brindabellas covered the warm earth of the plains. It dispersed by mid-morning as they approached Gurrangorambla Creek, which marked the eastern boundary of their lease. The leading horses baulked at the black bog edging the shallow water. One of the stockmen turned upstream, peering intently at the ground as he rode, following the wild horses' trail. He returned to the waiting men, pointing further along the stream.

'Brumby, he crosses up there. He smells the bog, knows how deep it is. We cross up there, eh?'

The crossing chosen by the wild horses of Currango Plains proved firm and safe.

It was difficult to know exactly where their leases started and finished, but it didn't seem to matter. The cattle and sheep would spread out for the next five months and the stockmen would stay with them, following them and camping close to where they fed. They would each reclaim their animals when, mustered into makeshift drop-log yards in Autumn, they would be drafted for the homeward run.

They unloaded supplies from the packhorses and stored them in a single roomed tin hut — something like an oversized toilet — they found in the centre of the lease. During the next week, temporary log shelters sprung up among the trees along Gurrangorambla Creek.

At night, they yarded the sheep into makeshift breaks and lit fires to ward off the dingoes, but during the day they couldn't prevent the sheep from wandering through the many bogs, so they took Jim Elemore's advice and laid bluestone around salt logs. The sheep's feet became impregnated with the bluestone as they walked through it to lick the precious salt.

The first fortnight on Currango came to an end and with it, Ellie and Nan prepared for their return journey. Joe made the decision who should remain with the stock and who should return to Boboyan.

'James, you go back with Ellie. Dad, you should return to Melvale.' Joe winked at Ellie as he said: 'Walter, I'll need you here with me to shepherd the sheep, and Jack has already said he'll stay on as cook.'

Ellie was drinking from a water bag when Walter singled her out.

'I was hoping I'd be coming back with you, Ellie.'

She lowered the canvas bag and looked up at the young man on horseback.

'You'd be more use up here, Walter. I'll see you at the end of Summer.'

Awkwardly, he shifted position in his saddle. Ellie gripped the wooden handle firmly and tilted the bag towards her mouth again.

'Ellie, I don't want you going off with no other bloke till I get back.'

She wiped the moisture from her lips with the back of her hand.

'Oh, believe me, Walter, I have no intention of going off with any bloke.'

'It's just that ... well ... I like you Ellie, and I want to have a decent crack at courting you.'

She shouldn't have, but Ellie laughed.

'I'm flattered that you care, Walter, but I'm not looking for a suitor. I'm too busy with Grassy Creek to even think about being courted.'

She felt sorry for the thin man as he rode away from her, but she would only consider courting if she met someone she respected. She wished Joe weren't her brother, for he was the only man she knew who came anywhere near her high standards.

She pushed the stopper back in the water bag and mounted Freckles.

*****

CHAPTER TEN

I opened the envelope, noticing the postmark from Canberra.

The Kosciusko Huts Association

acknowledging your assistance with the Project

cordially invites you to an Open Day at the

Thompson Family Homestead

GRASSY CREEK

Namadgi National Park

to celebrate the conservation of the building

Saturday 12 October 2002

10.30am to 3.30pm

Opening Speech by special guest

Mrs Tilly Anderson at 2pm

BYO Lunch and drinks

Scrawled on the bottom was the message:

"Hope you can make it. Norman."

I clicked the kettle on to boil, moved to the sunny end of my deck, and read the invitation again. Of course, there was no doubt that I would accept. Namadgi occupied a very special corner in my heart, and my heart dearly wanted to be there again.

The kettle whistled. I returned to the kitchen and savoured the aroma as the boiling water flooded the coffee grounds. I collected a notepad and pen and wrote my reply.

Dear Norman,

Nothing would give me greater pleasure than to attend the open house day at Grassy Creek Homestead. I look forward to renewing the friendships I formed over the work party weekends. I hope you are well.

Warm regards

Fran McMillan

There was only a week until the open house. To live alone is to live with the freedom to up and go whenever you wish. I went downstairs and covered the partly-made chairs, replaced my tools on the shadow board and locked my workshop door.

I loaded my car with tent, sleeping bag and camp stove, then ran up the stairs two at a time and threw a motley collection of t-shirts and shorts into my kit bag. I selected my best pair of jeans and my smartest button-up shirt for the special occasion. I made a few quick phone calls: one to my mother who always wants to know where I am — just in case; one to my sister to let her know where I would be — just in case; and one to a friend to look after my house while I was away. Then I sent an e-mail to Kelvin:

See you at Grassy Creek?

I signed it: Love, Fran. I didn't wait for a reply.

By teatime, I was ready to go. I resisted the temptation to leave immediately and went to bed. But sleep wouldn't come. I relived every moment of that lovely time in April.

*****

Ellie and James crossed over Pheasant Pass and cantered down the slope. An excitable black and white pup zigzagged its way home between the horses. Naas Valley seemed strangely empty without the stock — except for the turkeys. They had proved a great success and as the flock increased in number to a couple of hundred, Ellie had asked Nan to become a partner in the project.

Next day, the two women encouraged the squirming mass of birds to flutter and scramble across to the northern bank of Naas Creek.

With the valley now completely clear of stock, Ellie and Nan rode along the southern bank flicking wax matches into the grass for the trickleburn as they made their way back to their homesteads.

For the next few months, James rode the boundaries of the lease repairing fences and ring-barking trees to encourage the spread of grasses. He enjoyed being alone: setting traps for rabbits and wild dogs; cutting hollows in logs, then dragging them into position ready to fill with salt for next season's muster; ever alert for amorous tiger snakes seeking mates.

Every six weeks he rode out to Currango Plains with fresh supplies for Joe and Roger. During these visits, the men took a break from the monotony of shepherding. They rode past Currango Homestead to the western boundaries of the plains. There they stayed a couple of nights at Rules Point Hotel, getting very drunk with other pastoralists who had brought their stock from all parts of New South Wales for high summer grazing.

There were other patrons at the hotel. Well-heeled medical specialists from Sydney, who employed some of the pastoralists to show them the best spots to catch brown trout along Gurrangorambla Creek and Murrumbidgee River. Their behaviour around the Rules Point bar would have shocked their high-society patients back in Macquarie Street.

After a couple of days, sore but not at all sorry, Joe and Roger returned to their shepherding duties — dagging, wigging and crutching the sheep; guarding and branding new calves — while James rode back to Boboyan.

During the men's absence, Ellie scrubbed Grassy Creek, whitewashed the fireplaces and stove recess and polished the brass tap on the fountain. She added new clay between the chimney stones and to the interlaced twigs of wattle on her bedroom wall, then tilled the vegetable garden and dug cow manure into the freshly turned earth. She planted new cabbages, potatoes, carrots, turnips... She had hoped Yenohan would return to help out, but she had not been seen this Summer.

Ellie took yards of cotton lace fabric from her storage chest and made curtains for the living room windows. She hung them and gathered them with gold silk cord that she had bought from the travelling Indian hawker.

Joe and his stockmen left Currango for the return journey on the first of May. An early fall of snow made the passage difficult. They accepted the local knowledge of Jim Elemore and returned through the Murrumbidgee valley, but it was far from an easy route. Mile after mile of soft snow needed to be tramped flat by the horses and cattle to enable the sheep to proceed up the steep gullies to the ridge above Paytens Creek. They took the fall into Paytens gully in one go, for once they started on the downward slope, there was no chance of pulling up until they hit bottom. They followed the narrow valley to Murrumbidgee River, but the sheep, heavy with wool, refused to swim across.

The men swam the cattle across the ford, then constructed a makeshift bridge of logs and branches for the sheep. The bedraggled mob finally arrived in Boboyan valley knowing that fresh sweet grass awaited them underneath the snow.

Joe and James took off one hundred of the fattest cattle and sold them at the Cooma sales. They stayed in the township a week, socialising and shopping; enjoying the company of people other than stockmen for the first time in five months.

Meanwhile, Ellie prepared the house for Winter. She harvested the last of the cabbages and hung them high in the provisions hut with their outside leaves folded around their crisp hearts. She stacked the wood hut to its roof, then rode over to Davies' homestead to help Nan and John drench their cattle.

She watched the twin haloes around the sun every day for a week. The night before Joe and James arrived back at Grassy Creek, white mare's tails streaked across the sky from the west, precursors of the six inches of snow that fell that night.

*****

October is a beautiful time to travel. Neither hot nor cold and rarely raining. I arrived at Mount Clear campground on the Tuesday and spent the rest of the week walking over memories. The nights were still freezing; they probably always were up there, no matter what the season. A young couple was camped on the other side of the clearing. We waved, but respected each other's space.

Late on Friday afternoon I settled by the fire, weary from my day's walking along the Boboyan valley. I gave the sunset its full due. The sun was putting on this show, today, for me.

As daylight slipped beneath night, a pair of headlights split the darkness. They swung around and came to rest next to my car. The lights went out and the bush appeared all the darker for their absence. I heard the familiar creak of the Cruiser's door; heard the crunch of gravel under boot. A pair of legs appeared in the glow of the fire.

'Hello Fran.'

Kelvin's face was wide open in a smile.

'G'day. Want to share my fire?' I giggled.

He rolled a log beside me with his foot.

'Yeah, don't mind if I do.'

A long pause.

'So, how've you been, Fran? Your e-mails don't give away much?'

'Neither do yours! I've been busy making some chairs.'

'Yes, you told me that. But how have *you* been?'

'Well, I can't complain, I suppose. Life's not much different from when I last saw you.'

I had spent the whole week hoping beyond hope Kelvin would be here, and now he was, I was lost for words.

'And life in Canberra?'

'Oh, much the same. Nothing's changed.'

I steered the conversation onto easier ground: 'Well, it should be a lovely day tomorrow. Tell me, who's Tilly Anderson, do you know?'

'She's one of the Thompsons, the daughter of Joseph — although there's some confusion because she also seems to be tied up with Eleanor. We'll no doubt find out tomorrow.'

'I suppose the whole gang will be there?'

'The work party?'

I nodded.

'As far as I know. It would be unusual for any of them to miss an Open Day, after all the effort they've put in.'

We boiled the billy for tea, and Kelvin unwrapped a fruit cake from its foil. We shared supper, but my teeth began to chatter with the cold.

'I'm going to bed, Kelvin, just as soon as I've finished this. It's freezing.'

'Ni'night Fran. I'll sit here a while. It's been a long time since I've seen a good fire.'

I rose. 'Okay, ni'night then.'

I ruffled his hair as I passed, and he patted my bottom.

The silk lining of my sleeping bag chilled my bare skin as I crawled inside and pulled the hood over my ears.

In the still silence of midnight, the zipper to my tent slid open, tooth by tooth. From the dim glow of the dying fire outside, I saw Kelvin crawl in on his knees, then slowly close the zipper. I felt the gentle stroking of his hand on my hair. I folded back my sleeping bag. He undressed. His body was warm from the fire and from passion as he lay down beside me. He suckled my breast and his hand followed the curve of my back, stroking, caressing. My body ached with need as he entered me.

We lay contented and close; no gap between our bodies. My ear, resting on his chest, picked up the gradual slowing of his heartbeat.

'Damn you Fran McMillan,' he whispered into the darkness.

'Why? What do you mean?'

'I'd hoped it was only lust, and I could control that. But it's not. I love you.'

'Why so resentful.'

'Because I don't know what to do about it.'

I thought: you could leave your wife and live with me, but then I wasn't sure what I wanted either.

'Let's not worry about it tonight. Live for the moment,' I said, but I knew how inept my words sounded.

As we drifted off to sleep, I said: 'I love you too'.

*****

In the light of a new morning, our lives had changed. Love had woven threads that bound us. I knew I held a position in his life that was separate and whole, and I no longer felt the intruder into Kelvin and Maggie's marriage.

After breakfast, I packed my camping gear into my car and followed Kelvin to Grassy Creek.

We drove through the gate, wide open to welcome the visitors for the day, and arrived at nine-thirty. The paddock in front of the pine trees was already full of vehicles, mostly utes and four-wheel drives.

And what a joy to see the hut we had worked on seven months before. It stood proudly centre stage, knowing it was the star performer: new guttering; Mike's casement windows; the exterior walls stained a reddish-brown; and lace curtains framing each window. The front door was open in welcome.

I saw familiar faces from the work party scattered throughout the crowd: Norman, Mike, Geoff and Gloria, each animatedly describing some aspect of the restoration process for which they felt personally responsible.

'We'd better let the boss know we're here.'

Kelvin nodded to the right of the building where a dynamo in a shabby hat was spinning from group to group. Norman paused midflight when he saw us approaching and, with arms spread wide and crooked teeth flashing, gave Kelvin a bear hug, then turned to me.

'I'm sooo pleased you could make it, girlie.'

The hug he gave me was only slightly less boisterous than the one he bestowed on Kelvin.

'Gosh, Norman. You know I wouldn't have missed this for the world. The hut looks beautiful.'

'This is how she would have looked in her heyday. Mrs Anderson is delighted. She says it's mostly as she remembers it.'

He pointed to a lady standing proudly by the door, waiting to show visitors around her old home. She was a handsome, commanding woman, probably in her late seventies, dressed in tan trousers and a purple blouse, with hints of red amongst her greying hair, and a velvety olive skin.

'Could I meet her?' I asked.

'Of course. That's what she's here for,' replied Norman.

I left the two men to catch up, and went over to the verandah.

'Hello. You're Tilly Anderson, aren't you?'

'Yes, my dear. And who are you?'

'I'm Fran McMillan.'

We shook hands firmly.

'I had the pleasure of working on your hut earlier in the year. It's stayed with me ever since.'

'Please, come in and have a look around.'

She disappeared through the door. I followed.

I pointed to the interior wall separating the living room from the front bedroom: 'See that wall? I replaced that. Well, with some help from my friend Kelvin.'

I could no longer see the old nail holes and flaking patchwork of colour beneath its fresh coat of cream paint. We wandered through a doorway to the kitchen. New iron was nailed to the floor around the fireplace. The lean-to bedroom, off the kitchen, had sheets of clear perspex screwed over the wattle and daub walls. It was obvious some of the interweaving sticks had been ripped from the wall, probably by cold campers helping themselves to easy firewood. Now it was safe, but still visible to those who had only ever read of such construction.

'How do you feel, being here again?' I asked Tilly.

'Mostly good. It'll always be home to me. It does bring it all back though. The good memories with the bad.'

Then she looked at me intently with her penetrating brown eyes.

'It seems to me you care about this place, don't you.'

It was more of a statement than a question.

'I care for it deeply,' I replied. 'I haven't been able to get it out of my mind since I left in April. Especially the way Nola died. Having to be buried here all alone.'

'She's not alone any more,' replied Tilly. 'They say she was a mighty strong woman. I wish I'd known her. She died before I was born, of course.'

'Her ghost is still here,' I said.

'They're all still here: Nola, Eleanor, James, Joseph, Yenohan.'

'Who's Yenohan?' I hadn't heard this name mentioned before.

Tilly opened her mouth to reply just as a group noisily entered the front door. I saw her shoulders droop as she exhaled the air that contained the answer to my question.

'Do you want to escape the crowd?' I asked.

She nodded and hooked her arm through my elbow. We left by the back door as sightseers entered the kitchen to admire the stone wall surrounding the fireplace.

Tilly steered me up the rise behind the house. When we reached the gravesite, I noticed it looked different. The work party had found time to restore Nola's grave. The fence now stood upright and the rest of the hawthorn had been cleared, revealing two more graves. Tilly watched me intently as I looked at them.

'They're my parents,' she said.

*****

Yellow flames winked as they passed small gaps on their circular journey around the oven. A leg of lamb rested in its juices on a plate above the stove, filling the Thompson home with its seductive aroma. Ellie stirred the thickening gravy in the roasting pan then poured it into a white china gravy boat.

She summoned her brothers from the lounge: 'Dinner's ready, you two!'

Brothers and sister ate their evening meal, but Ellie noticed Joe was agitated. He only picked at his plate.

'I'd better go up Mount Clear tomorrow and check on the cattle,' he said.

'I wouldn't worry about them, Joe. They'll move down to lower ground,' replied James.

They continued eating. The blanket of new snow exaggerated the silence outside the dwelling and within.

After dinner, Joe walked onto the verandah and pulled the front door closed behind him. Ellie wrapped her shawl around her shoulders and followed. The moon was two days beyond full and its perfect roundness had begun to flatten. It illuminated the countryside in a ghostly blue-white sheen. The snow gum beyond the house threw the hint of a shadow across the field.

Ellie saw a small circle of red glow then fade at the far end of the verandah as Joe drew on his pipe. She perched on the rail enjoying the pungent smell of the tobacco: she had missed it since Roger was no longer around. Joe inverted his pipe and tapped it on the railing. The spent tobacco sizzled on the snow. He repacked the bowl with his thumb.

'What's wrong Joe?'

'What do you mean?'

'You've been distracted all evening. And that comment about the cattle on Mount Clear — you know they'll be okay. They always have been.'

Joe struck a match. It flared, and his red beard shimmered in the orange glow. He didn't speak again until the new tobacco smouldered steadily.

'It's something I can't talk about, Ellie.'

'We don't have any secrets, Joe Thompson!'

'I'm afraid we do Ellie. I'd tell you if I could, believe me, but this is my problem and I need to work it out for myself.'

A soft sucking noise from Joe's pipe put a full stop to the conversation. Ellie shivered in the cold beauty of the night.

'Go inside Ellie, I'll be all right. I'll head up the mountain tomorrow, but I'll be back on Sunday for dinner. Promise.'

As Ellie opened the door, he added: 'Thanks for caring, Sis'.

Ellie cleared the table, rolled the napkins away in their leather rings, shook the crumbs from the cloth and replaced it in the sideboard drawer until Sunday.

Joe's mood disturbed her as she washed the dishes. In her twenty-five years she had always had direct access to his thoughts. She had no idea what could be causing him such concern. His demeanour was no lighter the next day as he saddled Whisper and left for Mount clear after lunch.

Late in the afternoon Ellie looked towards the mountain expecting to see smoke rising from Joe's chimney. It was nearly dark and he should have reached his hut by now. But there was no smoke. Perhaps he needed to chop more firewood.

The next morning Ellie went to the wood hut to restock the firebox and looked towards the mountain again, but there was still no sign of smoke. She dropped the firewood in the snow and hurried to the old hut, flinging open the door.

'James! Something's happened to Joe!'

James's head appeared from beneath the grey woollen blanket.

'He's gone up Mount Clear to check on the cattle.'

'His chimney's not smoking. He wouldn't have slept without a fire. Not in this weather!'

James threw the blanket from his body and grabbed his trousers from the back of the chair next to his bed. He paused in his long underwear, staring at his big sister. She turned her back and he continued to dress.

'We'd better get help,' he said as he tucked his shirt into the waistband and hitched the braces over his shoulders.

Ellie was in the stables saddling Freckles before James had pulled on his boots. They galloped over Pheasant Pass to the Davies' house. Nan saw them approaching and met them in the front yard. She knew by Ellie's eyes something was amiss.

'Joe's missing!' Ellie shouted from her saddle, as Freckles circled in response to her panic.

A missing horseman in the high country is to be taken seriously.

'John and Steven'll go with you, I'll go and get the Robinsons,' Nan shouted over her shoulder as she headed for her tackroom.

The horses lunged through the spin drift that had obliterated Whisper's tracks. The search party fanned out and had covered the distance between Grassy Creek and the foot of Mount Clear by lunchtime, peering behind every rock and tree, over every steep drop.

They regrouped in the lea of a house-sized rock of granite. Nan had brought some bully beef and bread and insisted they all eat something. Ellie couldn't bring herself to take food, but she knew that the others needed sustenance, so she walked in circles around them until they had eaten their lunch.

Once on Mount Clear, they spread out again. Around three o'clock a sharp whistle reached Ellie's ears. She forced Freckles on, cruelly ignoring his effort as he sank to his girth with each step.

Nan had found Whisper waiting quietly by a broad-based candlebark a mile from Joe's hut. His reins were trailing on the ground, waiting for the next instruction from his master, as he had been trained to do. His saddle, bridle, stirrups were all in place. There was no sign of anything amiss.

Ellie saw a pair of moleskin-clad legs walking towards her through the undergrowth. She let out the breath she had been holding since breakfast and the grip eased on her skull.

But it wasn't Joe. It was John Davies.

'I'm afraid it's bad news, Ellie.'

He walked over and patted her knee with one hand, and stroked Freckles' neck with the other. Then he turned and walked back through the bush. Everyone dismounted and followed.

Yenohan sat swaying, moaning, on a rock. She heard the approach of boots crunching through the snow, and melted into the trees.

Joe lay on his back, one leg bent double beneath him, an arm across his belly, his eyes staring blankly. A rivulet of blood froze in its path from his skull, smashed against a hard rock. His hat and stock-whip lay on the far side of the rock. Ellie knelt down and gently picked up his head and laid it on her lap, oblivious of his blood on her hands and her trousers.

James made a sled from fallen timber and tied a grey woollen blanket from Joe's hut to the thick branches. He towed his brother's body down the mountain. Ellie followed, leading Whisper. The rest of the Boboyan folk trailed helplessly.

On the rise beyond the house, next to their mother, Ellie and James laid Joe to rest as Grassy Creek pushed its flooded waters towards the roaring Murrumbidgee River.

*****

The last of the visitors' cars swept out of the paddock.

'Well, the old girl's on her own now,' said Norman as he pulled the front door. He looked from Kelvin to me: 'Not that it's any of my business, but are you two okay?'

'Yeah, probably,' replied Kelvin. Norman then looked at me. I shrugged my shoulders, not sure what to say.

'Well, if you need a shoulder, give us a ring.' He patted Kelvin fondly on the back then hugged me.

'Look after yourself, girlie. I hope you'll get in touch if you're ever back down this way.'

I promised I would, and he climbed into his ute and leaned out the window: 'Don't forget to padlock the gate, we wouldn't want the place trashed after all the work we've put into it,' and drove off, his arm waving out the window.

'Are we okay?' Asked Kelvin.

'Okay by me,' I said, and snuggled into his side.

Now that we were alone, Kelvin put his arm around me and walked me to my car.

'I suppose I will need to get my life in order now, Fran. It may take some time, though. Do you reckon you can wait?'

'I'm unlikely to get a better offer,' I ribbed. 'Yes, of course I'll wait. Just don't let it be any longer than necessary. Please.'

We kissed goodbye. I had no idea when I would see him again.

We drove back north: Kelvin to Canberra, me to Brisbane.

*****

On the banks of the Brungle River, Yenohan lay on a bed of soft ferns as the old black midwife stroked her belly. Her time was near. Mooroo hovered nearby, ready to help her daughter give birth to this mystery baby. Yenohan held her secret and her grief close as she sweated and writhed. That evening, a little girl slid from between her legs, filled her lungs with air and yelled.

*****

CHAPTER ELEVEN

Rain clouds were gathering in the west. That was good: the tinder dry country was crying out for rain. All day they massed darkly above the mountain peaks that poked into their billowing bellies.

The earth held its breath.

But the clouds didn't deliver rain. Instead, they delivered forty-four lightning strikes within the next twenty-four hours. From the western slopes of Kosciusko to the Brindabellas fires caught and smouldered: a tree here, a paddock of grass there. The storms passed, dragging a strong westerly breeze behind them. Slowly to begin with, each fire began its eastward journey. The breeze quickened. The flames leaped higher.

During the second night some of the fires joined and their excitement grew. Another dry storm blew through. Fire fed fire.

Day by day the fires merged until, by the seventh day, the forty-four fires had become one vast conflagration that generated its own electrical storm as it rushed headlong towards Canberra, turning the air a weird orange colour.

Huts, lovingly restored, stood in its way.

*****

Kelvin switched on the radio. It was already tuned to his station of choice.

'... this is 104.7. The time is seven fifteen. And it's a hot one here in Canberra where the temperature is already 35 degrees. We're having trouble reaching the Emergency Services Bureau, so if any listeners have updates on the bushfire situation, could you please ring the station ...'

Kelvin mopped his forehead as he listened. For a couple of weeks now, the fires had been burning out of control in the national parks. He had rung Norman to see if any of the huts were in danger. No one had any way of knowing. The fire was too severe. The park was closed.

He walked out onto the back verandah of his home in the suburb of Chapman. The heat hit his face. The entire western sky was a wall of smoke fifteen kilometres away.

He looked to his right. Everyone was out watching. Words of optimism bounced from verandah to verandah. They were okay. Even if the fire did come, the pine forest was nearly a kilometre away, and there was a field of grass between it and them. And the Equestrian Centre. A good buffer.

At one o'clock the radio announcer's voice was rising in tandem with the temperature. His words came more rapidly, his shallow breathing was audible: 'the pine forest on Mount Stromlo is ablaze and the suburb of Duffy will be the next to go.'

Kelvin froze. Duffy was the other side of Hindmarsh Drive, less than two kilometres away. The sun pushed its sickly orange glow through the darkness that filled the early afternoon air.

He grabbed his phone and rang Maggie's mobile number. She had stayed away overnight without phoning. Again. He cursed her absence. As she answered, he bellowed into the mouthpiece: 'Get home! Now!'

Kelvin ran to the garden shed and grabbed the extension ladder. From the roof, he could see the full horror. It was terrifyingly beautiful. A wall of flames thirty metres high roared towards him with the sound of a screaming jet. Black, thick smoke billowed above the flames. He thought he could hear explosions.

He had blocked the down pipes with Maggie's tennis balls and was filling the gutters with water when a silver BMW skidded into the driveway. Maggie sprang from her car and grabbed a rake and hose and began extinguishing the small fires erupting all around the garden as the pine bark mulch caught and smouldered. On the roof,

Kelvin saturated his boots, shorts, shirt, head. The water sizzled as it touched his skin.

A house in the next street was the first to go. The flames flew at it horizontally.

Houses started popping: gas bottles; paint stored in garden sheds; cars; a fire truck; all swallowed by the fire's fury.

A sulphur crested cockatoo landed at Maggie's feet, still burning, but she couldn't hear her own screaming above the roar. Electricity poles dangled from their wires, their bases burnt through. The brown and orange air flashed blue as the wires touched.

Rising above the din, an eerie continuous wail came from the radio accompanied by a voice that didn't seem quite human, issuing instructions for evacuation. A police car drove slowly along the street, its headlights unable to penetrate the blackness. Loud speakers told the residents to evacuate. Kelvin yelled at them to get fucked.

Numbly, people abandoned their burning houses to help their neighbours who still had a chance.

That night in Brisbane, Fran McMillan stared at the television screen in her living room; hugging a cushion; horrified by the images of houses on fire, roads choked with cars, people on roofs pointing pathetically trickling hoses at the monster.

She reached for the phone and dialled Kelvin's home number. But there was no answer. She tried his mobile. She tried Norman. Nothing.

'... the City of Canberra is without power, sewerage, and phones ... four people have died, and nearly five hundred houses have been destroyed by the worst natural disaster known to Australia. The most heavily affected areas are Duffy and Chapman ...'

For three days Fran tried in vain to contact Kelvin. On the fourth, she threw some clothes in her car and headed south.

*****

PART THREE

...

CHAPTER TWELVE

After the good years of '25 and '26, the dry Summer of 1927 came as a shock to the pastoralists of Boboyan. Ellie and James struggled to keep their stock fed, moving them from valley to valley, seeking out the best of the worst, each grieving for Joe in their own way.

It was pointless making the journey to Currango Plains that Summer: Currango Homestead's manager Ted Brassil was even bringing his stock down to the valleys in search of feed.

The Boboyan families pulled together as usual, although Ellie noticed a cooling of relations between the Thompsons and the Robinsons since the time she discouraged Walter's amorous overtures. And she was annoyed with Yenohan. Ellie had grown to depend on her friend's help around the place, cooking for the extra hands at mustering time, but she hadn't seen her since Joe died his lonely death on Mount Clear over two years before.

Nineteen twenty-eight began just as dry. Grassy Creek had stopped flowing and was now a string of muddy puddles between the tussock clumps. James had assembled the few surviving pitiful sheep ready to take north to Melvale.

Ellie was bucketing her bath water onto the cabbages when she heard the sound of shuffling footsteps behind her. She turned around to see Yenohan standing with her weight on her right leg, her left foot propped on her right knee, her right hand firmly holding onto a very small girl with big brown eyes and auburn hair.

'G'day Ellie.'

Ellie sank onto the log bordering the garden.

'Oh, dear God!'

She looked from the woman to the little girl, trying to make sense of the picture before her.

'This here's Matilda.'

Yenohan tried to push the toddler forward, but she clung to her mother's hand, refusing to budge.

'Matilda?'

Ellie shook her head in disbelief. All she could see was Joe's face looking back at her. Yenohan picked up the squirming child and, approaching Ellie, held out her daughter. Ellie took the little girl into her arms.

'What does this mean, Yenohan? You and Joe!?'

Yenohan squatted flat-footed, looking down at the ground, pushing leaves around with a twig and nodded. Ellie had lived with Yenohan and Joe, had watched them laugh together, ride horses, work on the plains. She hadn't the slightest inkling that her brother and Yenohan had been any more than friends. Then Ellie remembered how Joe had kept to himself on his mountain and of his unspoken troubles the night before he had ridden to his death. She now knew that Yenohan had not returned to her people at Brungle Mission each Winter as she had thought.

'Was it over the Winters?'

Yenohan nodded again.

'Yes Ellie. And sometimes the summers. With my hair short, other cattlemen thought I was a boy, so I could ride with him.' She stopped pushing the stick around the dirt and looked up at Ellie. 'I loved him, Ellie, and he loved me.'

Ellie kept shaking her head, her eyes closed, trying to understand. She felt anger at her brother, and at Yenohan.

'Come inside, Yenohan. We need to talk.'

Ellie strode off into the kitchen, carrying the girl on her hip. She placed her on a chair. Matilda twisted on the seat, whimpering, searching for her mother. Ellie pulled out a chair for Yenohan.

'Why on earth didn't you tell me?'

Ellie's eyes bored into the head of black curls bowed before her. The full shame of the relationship that had driven Joe and Yenohan to keep it a secret showed in Yenohan's body.

'You just disappeared! Without a word!'

When Yenohan finally lifted her head, her eyes were bloodshot with controlled tears.

'Joe asked me not to say anything, but when he died and I had the baby, I thought you'd be good and mad. You'd not understand.'

Ellie thought she had known her brother better than anyone. It turned out she barely knew him at all.

'Did Joe know about Matilda?'

'Yes, Ellie. I told him I'm expecting a baby after the trip to Currango. Just before he died. We was going get married.'

'Why have you come back here now?' asked Ellie.

'The welfare fella's been asking questions. He sees her red hair and wants to take her. He doesn't think I should have a half-white kid. You reckon I could stay here for a bit, Ellie?'

'Yes. Yes, of course you can.'

Ellie walked around the table to her niece, and squatted in front of her. Matilda squeezed her eyes shut, then laughed.

'What does your mob make of her?'

'They don't like her being white. Reckon I should've married a black man. But Mum and Dad think she's okay.'

Ellie lifted Matilda from the chair and went into the leanto bedroom off the kitchen. She deposited Matilda on one of the single beds and went to fetch clean sheets from a cupboard. Yenohan took the bundle from Ellie and made up the other bed.

When they had finished, they returned to the kitchen table.

'Stay as long as you want, Yenohan. I could do with help, and the company. James is heading off to Melvale with the sheep next week.'

'Thanks Ellie.'

Yenohan pulled a pipe from a large pocket of her floral dress and a tin of tobacco from another. Ellie recognised it as Joe's pipe. With practised hands, Yenohan filled the bowl, packing the tobacco tightly with her thumb, then lit it; but she couldn't stop the tears overflowing the pink rim of her eyes.

*****

I arrived in Canberra around lunchtime and drove slowly along Kelvin's street in Chapman. It had been five days since the fires hit Canberra, and I hadn't heard from him.

I gagged at the devastation. House after house had been burnt. Occasionally a brick garage rose alone, silent sentinel to the catastrophe. Then in the middle of it, unbelievably, one house had escaped unscathed.

The street was black. Every tree, every post, the acres of grass behind the back fences; and beyond, stretching to the horizon, black tree trunks bristled up the slope of Mount Stromlo like a gigantic smouldering dead animal.

But without letterboxes, I had no way of knowing which of these allotments would have been Kelvin's. I pulled into the gutter and walked the rest of the street in an uncomfortable daze of disbelief, then I turned to go back to my car. This was other people's grief. I didn't belong here.

A green Fiat stopped in the middle of the street. A young woman peered through the passenger window at me. I gave her a half-hearted smile and continued walking. She pulled into the curb and stepped from her car, leaning against the open door.

'Fran? It is Fran, isn't it? Fran McMillan?'

I looked at this stranger.

'Yes. I'm sorry, do I know you?'

She closed her door and walked over to me.

'No, you don't know me. I'm Kelvin's daughter, Trudie.'

I knew my mouth was wide open. I couldn't shut it.

'I thought it was you. I recognised you from a photo near Dad's computer.'

She pointed across the street.

'That's their house. Or at least, where it was. Nothing left now. I can't even find any memories.'

She crossed the street and I followed.

Bricks and roofing steel lay in a jumble of what was recognisably once a house. It smelt of death — the death of a home.

Trudie laid a hand on my arm. 'Dad's told me all about you, Fran. Don't feel embarrassed. I'm on your side.'

She wasn't all that much younger than me. Early thirties perhaps. She had her father's black hair (without the touches of grey) and his hazel eyes.

She linked her arm through mine and said: 'Come on, let's get out of here. It's not going to do either of us any good sifting through this. I live in the next suburb. Where's your car?'

It suddenly occurred to me that I hadn't said a word since she introduced herself.

'Trudie, is Kelvin okay?'

'Physically? Yep. He wasn't hurt in the fire. Emotionally, he's vulnerable. He's still in shock.'

'My car's down at the corner.'

'Follow me. We'll go and put the kettle on and we can talk.'

We left the bleak streets of Chapman and drove into leafy Fisher. So close, but no damage. The fire had somersaulted over her suburb and speared Mount Taylor to the east.

Trudie wheeled into her driveway, between two brick gateposts. It was a typical Canberran home: solid brick; twin garages under the verandah on the right; brick steps leading to the door on the left; with three chimneys growing out of a green tiled roof. One of the garage doors opened as she approached and her Fiat disappeared inside. She opened the second garage door and waved me in.

She gathered her shopping from the back seat, passing a bag of vegies to me, then closed the garage doors. At the top of the internal staircase she kicked off her shoes, nudged a red and green plastic tip truck out of the way and walked down the hallway.

'Put them on the bench, Fran. I'll get the kettle.'

She flicked the kettle on then groped inside her handbag for her cigarettes and lighter, and walked out through sliding glass doors onto the back patio.

'You smoke?' She asked, offering her packet. I shook my head.

'No thanks, Trudie.'

'You're wise. Take a seat.'

She flopped onto a cane chair beside a round glass-topped table and spun another chair around for her feet.

'God, it's hot! Though to you, it's probably not that bad.'

She drew on the cigarette as if she was making love to it — head back, eyes closed — and wriggled her toes.

'This isn't uncomfortable. It's the humidity I can't stand,' I replied.

The kettle whistled in the kitchen.

'Tea?'

'Mmm. That'd be lovely.'

She emerged from the house with a tray: teapot, cups, strainer, sugar, milk, biscuits.

'Tell me Trudie, how much has Kelvin told you.'

She stubbed her cigarette out, then looked at me.

'He's in love with you. Actually, he didn't need to tell me that. When he came home from his walkies last April he was different. His eyes had life in them, it's been missing for some years, I figured then he'd probably met someone. He didn't say anything — not at first. But he had changed.

'He went back to working in his workshop under the house. He bought a super piece of red cedar and started making a dining room table — of all things! Beautiful. Thick turned legs. He hasn't used the lathe for years, but suddenly you couldn't get him away from it. When the fire came through, he wouldn't leave without that damn table. It just fitted in the back of the Cruiser.'

Kelvin knew I was making the cedar chairs. Was he making the table to go with them? I pushed the idea aside as romantic nonsense.

'Where is he now?' I asked.

'He's staying here. With us.'

Trudie lit up again.

'I shouldn't. It'll be the death of me.'

A child's voice yelled from the front as a screen door slammed. Two bundles of energy burst onto the verandah.

'Hey, you two. Steady on. We've got a visitor. Now, come and say hello to Fran.'

Two boys, about six and eight, stopped abruptly and said, in unison: 'Hello, Fran.'

Trudie put her hand on each boy's head in turn: 'This is Adam and this is Chris. Okay boys. Go and get changed. You can join us for afternoon tea.'

'Cool!'

A flurry of spindly legs disappeared into the house again.

'Have you got any kids, Fran?'

'A boy. He's fifteen. He turns sixteen this year.'

'Where's he?'

'He's in America with his father.'

'That's tough.'

We waited until Adam and Chris had drunk their juice and eaten their fill of biscuits. Trudie sent them off to play in the yard.

'Now, Fran. We should talk about you and Dad because, in my opinion, he needs a kick up the arse, so to speak. He tried to ignore his feelings for you when he came back in April, but every time you sent him an e-mail he had to face them all over again.'

'You seem close to your father.'

'Very close. I've known for years that he and Mum are just good mates who share a house, but he wouldn't see it. He can be a frustrating old bastard at times. Meeting you has made him come alive again.

'One day I cornered him in his workshop and said: "What's her name?". He kept planing the tabletop and, without looking up, said: "Fran". Then he 'fessed up and told me about your trip up Naas valley. Boy, I couldn't have been happier. Mum's had affairs. I'm sure Dad knows that. But he's always been too loyal to even look at another woman. You must be special, Fran McMillan.'

'I wouldn't say so.'

'Ah well, time'll tell. When the invite came for the opening of Grassy Creek, I knew he was hoping you'd be there. Then he showed me your e-mail. I said: "Of course, you're going, aren't you". He said: "Suppose I'd better". I said: "Bloody oath you'd better, even if I have to drag you there myself".'

It was impossible not to like this young woman. She had the straightforward attitude of her father, but a vivacity that oozed out of every pore. I suspected she owed that to Maggie.

Trudie rocked back on her chair.

'So, how come you're here now, Fran?'

'I haven't been able to contact Kelvin since the fires. No e-mails, and the phones seem to be down, even his mobile. I've been worried sick. I decided I'd better come and see for myself. I didn't expect to find such a horrible sight. It must be so difficult for the victims ... How's Maggie?'

'Survivors! Not victims! Mum's okay. She went to stay with some friends. We wanted her to stay here too, but she didn't want to be with the boys. She finds them overwhelming. Can't say I blame her, but I could've kept them quiet. Anyway, she'll be kept busy sorting out the insurance. Dad knows she'd take over anyway, so he's leaving it all up to her. I suspect he's reassessing his life, big time.'

I hoped so.

'Where're you staying?' She asked.

'I've only arrived today. I haven't given it any thought.'

'No arguments then, you're staying here!'

'Oh no, I couldn't. Thank you anyway Trudie.'

'Why not, Fran? There's heaps of room. I'll go and clear out the spare room. The kids use it as their toy room. Come and give us a hand.'

It was pointless to argue.

We went back down the internal stairs to a room off the garage. Trudie tossed me some sheets and a pillowcase then pushed the toys to one corner. As I was making up the daybed, I heard a car pull into the driveway and the garage door open.

'Ah, there's Stephen. He's my hubby.'

She opened the door leading into the garage: 'In here, love. We've got a visitor.'

A lovely bear of a man stooped through the doorway. He wore overalls heavily impregnated with grease.

'This is Fran,' said Trudie, a tad smugly, I thought.

'Not the Fran?'

'One and the same.'

It appeared this family shared its secrets.

Then I heard a diesel pull into the front yard. I looked at Trudie: 'Kelvin?'

She nodded.

'Go out and surprise him!'

I know I blushed.

I walked out through the open garage door and stood there. Kelvin was looking down at the passenger seat, gathering up some papers. He straightened up and saw me. He just sat staring through the windscreen.

Then he became a blur through my tears. I heard the door slam, hurried footsteps, papers blowing across the driveway; felt his arms holding me tight as he rocked me from side to side. I clung to him for dear life.

*****

CHAPTER THIRTEEN

Yenohan and Matilda stayed with Ellie over the Summer. As Matilda's laughter filled the home, Ellie grew to love her brother's child as if she were her own. Ellie and Yenohan took turns at cradling her in front of them on the saddle as they rode over the hills. Ellie taught her to look for caterpillars among the cabbage leaves. Yenohan took her to the old Wolgal camp on the banks of Grassy Creek and sang songs and told stories. This half-Thompson and half-Wolgal girl knew both worlds.

When the first fall of snow drifted over Grassy Creek, the wanderlust stirred in Yenohan. The coming of Winter in the mountains had always been the signal for the tribe's migration to warmer lands. Yenohan had ignored the call while Joe was there to love, but now her family would be getting ready for Winter at Brungle and Yenohan pined for her tin hut with its polished earthen floor and the happy noise of her brothers.

Ellie watched Yenohan's internal struggle for weeks, fearing she would leave and take Matilda with her. To Ellie, it would be like losing Joe all over again.

Finally, she addressed the problem.

'You want to go back to your mob, don't you, Yenohan.' It was more a statement than a question.

'Yes, Ellie. It's where I belong.'

'What about Matilda?'

Yenohan shook her head, fighting tears. Fighting fears.

'You could leave her here with me. She would be safe and I'd take good care of her. You know that.'

Yenohan lifted Matilda onto her hip and left the room, unable to face such a decision. She camped by the creek for a week with her daughter, sleeping by the fire at night, roaming the bush during the day. This little girl was her only link to the love she and Joe shared. She was part of her body, her mind, her soul. To take her back to her family would mean a very real risk of losing her forever, and that she could not bear. If Matilda remained with Ellie, the links with her white family would remain. Joe would have wanted this.

The question of Yenohan herself remaining with Ellie and Matilda did not arise. Yenohan was a Wolgal woman. She belonged with her people. Part of her heart died when she was apart from them.

Yenohan returned to the house, her decision made. She handed her child to her friend with an unspoken request for her to guard this treasure.

'I'll be back next Summer, Ellie.'

Whisper had led a quiet life around the house yard since Joe's death. He was nearing twenty, but remained in fine shape. It worried Ellie that this working horse might be bored with life. She placed Joe's saddle on his back and handed the reins to Yenohan.

'I think Whisper would appreciate a good ride, Yenohan. Take him back to Brungle with you.'

Yenohan rode towards the pass up to the high plains, staring backwards at the shimmering forms of Ellie and Matilda through her tears. When she could no longer make out their shapes in the shadow of the house, she turned and faced her journey.

*****

When James returned from Melvale with the winter supplies, Ellie closed Grassy Creek to the outside world and began the task of teaching her niece how to be a white child. She treadled her machine in the light from the window, creating little frocks trimmed with ribbon and lace. She made Matilda wait until they were all seated at the dinner table, then showed her how to remove the serviette from its leather keep and flick it onto her lap.

Ellie took Matilda to the rise beyond the house and, standing before the two graves, explained how Nola was her grandmother — like Mooroo — and how beautiful her father had been. But Matilda was more interested in picking the periwinkles that winked at her through the snow.

Ellie picked up Matilda: 'Perhaps it's too soon,' and she took her back to the warmth of the fire.

Towards the end of Winter, Constable Small from Cooma rode through Boboyan, doing his rounds. He was a less than bright fellow. He watched the little girl sitting on the other side of the table as he slurped his tea.

'Got quite dark skin, hasn't she?'

Ellie ruffled the red hair and answered: 'Yes, she is quite tanned. It must be her mother's Italian blood coming through.'

He laughed with an intake of air that could have been mistaken for a horse's snort. 'You sure she's not a half-caste?'

'Oh, very sure, Constable. My brother, Joe, married a beautiful Italian woman in Sydney. I believe she came from royal blood. Sadly, she died a year ago and I am the only living relative.'

Ellie hoped Matilda was too young to absorb this lie.

Puzzled, the policeman thanked her for the tea and rode off, not entirely sure he hadn't been taken for a fool.

Winter passed and the snows melted from the lower slopes of the mountain to dribble through the sphagnum moss. The dribble became a rill, the rill became a rivulet, the rivulet trickled over the bank into Grassy Creek.

The smell of tobacco drifted into the house ahead of Yenohan who appeared at the door, puffing on her pipe. Matilda immediately recognised this as her mother, and ran to the door and leapt onto Yenohan, wrapping her arms around her mother's neck and burying her head beneath her chin.

Yenohan's face opened wide in a grin as she said: 'G'day Ellie. I'm back.'

Ellie stood on the verandah in the darkness of evening and watched the olive trunks of the sallees dance to the fire by the creek. She listened to the low drone of Yenohan's storytelling, then the childish giggle that mingled with the throaty chuckle. Ellie didn't understand the Wolgal words of the songs they sang. She grew tired and went to bed, but in the morning she found Yenohan and Matilda's beds had not been slept in. She went to the creek side but the fire was cold.

When James returned to the homestead that evening, Ellie met him at the door, wringing her hands. Her appearance disturbed James: strands of hair had escaped their band and clung to her clammy cheeks.

'Yenohan's gone, and she's taken Matilda!'

James swung from his bay gelding and loosened the girth strap.

'Well, she is her mother.'

Ellie went inside to regain her composure. She washed her face and brushed her hair then set the table for dinner. She remained silent throughout the meal.

James placed his knife and fork in the centre of his plate and asked: 'What're you worried about Ellie?'

'Matilda's only three. She's too young to be out in the bush. There's dingoes, snakes, wild pigs, and she's got her good dress on. It'll get filthy.'

James stroked the black stubble on his chin with the back of his hand, a habit he'd developed since he became old enough to grow a beard. Amusement played around his black eyes.

'Where do you think she's lived for the first two-and-a-half years of her life? You might be trying to make her into a little white lady, but you'll have to face the fact that she's a little black girl.'

Ellie's cheeks flushed in anger.

'She's Joe's child as much as Yenohan's! She has a right to be a little white girl!'

'If I were you, Ellie, I'd let Matilda decide what she wants to be. And right now, it appears she wants to be with her mother.'

James excused himself from the table and lifted his hat down from the hat peg by the back door: 'Now, if you'll excuse me, I've got a heavy day tomorrow. I've got to get the sheep out of Pheasant. And if Yenohan's not back by morning, I could do with a hand.'

He walked over to the old hut to sleep the sleep of a hard-working pastoralist.

All week, Ellie and James worked on the muster. They filled the hollow logs with salt, then rounded up the woollies ready for the drive to Melvale. Each evening as Ellie returned, she looked for Matilda and Yenohan.

At the beginning of the second week she saw smoke rising from the chimney as they descended from Pheasant Hill. Matilda ran out to meet her, chattering in the Wolgal tongue. Yenohan chuckled at the look on Ellie's face.

'We talk whiteman talk here, Matilda.'

The young girl easily changed to broken English, then changed again to talk Aunt Ellie talk.

Yenohan spoke through her pipe: 'We've been walking in the bush. You want to round up them turkeys, Ellie? Move them over Grassy Creek to fresh grass?'

'Yes, Yenohan. We'll do it tomorrow.'

'Yes Ellie. We'll do it tomorrow.'

She relit her pipe and leant back on the chair, content with her lot.

*****

The evening meal vibrated with life. Seated between Kelvin and Trudie, I observed this family as happy conversation flew between stuffed mouths. I could see how, with such support and love, these people were indeed survivors, not victims of the previous week's disaster.

But I was exhausted. When I had finished my meal, I excused myself from the dinner table and retired to the bedroom downstairs. I lay listening to the night-time ritual being played out above me: Adam and Chris chasing each other back and forth in the hallway; Trudie running their bath; teeth-cleaning; the quiet drone of Stephen's deep voice reading from The Hobbit; then came two very soft taps on my door. Before I could respond, the door opened and Kelvin's head appeared.

'Anyone home?'

It suddenly occurred to me to feel embarrassed about being there.

Kelvin kicked off his shoes and lay on the bed next to me. Pulling me onto his chest, he stroked my hair. Neither of us spoke for a long time. I tuned in to his slow, rhythmic breathing. There were so many questions to be asked, so many answers to be questioned.

I broke the silence.

'Why didn't you answer your phone?'

'Which one? The one that burnt in the house, or the one I lost in the yard?'

'Oh! That was probably a silly question.'

I sat up and faced him: 'You could have rung me! I've been worrying myself sick. You must have known I'd hear about the fires! Or didn't I even cross your mind?'

'Believe me, Fran, you were plumb right in the middle of my mind. The truth is, I think I'm still in shock. Last Saturday morning I was picking up the *Times* from my front driveway and waiting for my toast to pop up. That same night I was homeless, wifeless, and lucky to be alive.'

'Wifeless? Why wifeless? What's happened?'

'I told Maggie about you the day before the fires. I told her we had to talk; to work out the future. She drove off, saying: "That's it, then", and didn't come home until I called her in a panic the next day. She's gone off again now, you know.'

He pulled me back against him, and resumed stroking my hair. I wished I had a key into his mind, wished I knew his innermost thoughts, but I suspected no-one but Kelvin knew them.

We lay together, not speaking, drawing comfort from one another. Through the daze of sleep, I heard the TV upstairs. When I awoke again, the house was silent, and Kelvin was snoring softly into my hair. I turned out the light.

The first rays of sunlight peeped under the door to the garage as we woke. Quietly, we made love, then Kelvin rose from the bed.

'Where are you going?' I whispered.

'Shhh,' he placed a finger against my lips.

'I want to be in my bed when Chris and Adam get up.'

'Okay. See you at breakfast then,' and I drifted back into a fitful sleep.

When I finally woke and went upstairs, Stephen had already left with the boys. Kelvin and Trudie were out on the verandah, drinking tea.

'Sleep okay?' Asked Trudie.

'No, not really. My mind kept busy.'

'It's the state all over Canberra this week.'

I turned to Kelvin.

'What about the Thompson's homestead? Have you heard anything?'

'No news yet. I've been trying to find out all week, but they can't send a reconnaissance team in till the fires have burnt themselves out.'

'I've gotta go to the recovery centre today. You two'll be all right?' asked Trudie.

'Yeah, we'll be all right,' replied Kelvin.

'What recovery centre?' I asked.

I helped Trudie clear away the breakfast dishes, then she prepared a lunch-box and coffee flask for herself as she explained: 'There's an old primary school at Lyons, a couple of suburbs away. Derelict. The government's converted it to an operational centre for now. It's somewhere for people to stay until they get their accommodation sorted. There's all sorts of services there: government departments and community groups. Centrelink has set up there to help people who can't get to their office. I'm a social worker with Centrelink. We're getting word out that anyone can drop in to the centre for anything they need.'

I felt like a fifth wheel. The people of this city needed to get on with their rehabilitation unhindered by onlookers.

'I suppose I should be heading back to Queensland, now that I know you're all right.'

I said the words, but I did not feel the conviction.

'Not so fast. What are you going back for?' asked Kelvin.

'I'm not sure. It was an impulsive move on my part coming down.'

'You could come with me,' said Trudie. 'We could sure do with a hand at the centre.'

'Okay. I'd love to.'

I turned to Kelvin: 'What about you?'

'Not today. I've stuff to sort out, but you go.'

Trudie snapped the lid on her lunch-box.

'That's it. We'll share my lunch. Be home with the boys about three-thirty, Dad, see you then.'

She reached up and kissed her father.

The recovery centre was abuzz. Mattresses covered the floor and kids lined up on plastic chairs, watching a television flickering under the row of casement windows. The adults, mostly women, leaned on a red laminex table drinking instant coffee from styrofoam cups, swapping stories. Their men were out in the streets helping to secure the areas of danger.

But despite the tragedy, there was laughter. Complete strangers were helping one another: looking after each other's children and making each other cups of tea. Precious family photos, in some instances the only possessions saved from the fire, were passed around.

It had only taken Canberrans thirty-six hours to get their lifeline into place: dispensing clothing; a place to sleep and contact relatives; money; comfort. I wondered how larger cities would cope with such an emergency.

Trudie set me up at a table and chair.

'As people come in, ask what it is they need, then direct them. As you can see, each government department has a sign on its desk. Any questions, I'll be over behind that screen.'

A steady stream of people came to me throughout the morning and I did my best to direct them.

I couldn't rid my nostrils of the acrid odour of smoke. Boxes full of clean clothes had been donated to the centre, and the people with whom I mixed had exchanged their sweat and smoke impregnated rags for them. They had showered and scrubbed their hair, but the smoke had a hold on their skin. Perhaps all of Canberra smelt that way.

Nearing lunch time, I joined some women at a trestle table and we converted the trays of sliced bread and boxes of salad into a mountain of sandwiches. With the atmosphere of a holiday camp, the children made short work of the crates of milk that were delivered. I worked in awe of such a positive mood.

At the end of a long day, we returned to Trudie's home with Kelvin's two lively grandsons bouncing around the back seat. A silver BMW was parked in the driveway. With the shout of 'Nan!' Adam and Chris rocketed from the car.

'Oh dear!'

Trudie put her hand on my arm: 'Now don't you worry. Dad knows we're due home about now. He could have choofed her off if he'd wanted to'.

'That doesn't stop me feeling awkward.'

'You've got to face her sometime.'

I followed Trudie up the front stairs, far outside my comfort zone.

'Hi Mum. How's it going?'

I hadn't expected such an attractive woman. She was shorter than I, not much over five feet, with smooth shoulder-length brown hair. I raked my fingers through my sweaty strands and wished I had washed them, or at least twisted them into a knot. She held out a firm tanned arm around which two slim gold bangles tinkled.

'You must be Fran.'

No "pleased to meet you"!

I shook her hand and searched her well-made-up face for signs of friend or foe. Then her eyes smiled.

'Kelvin's told me all about you.'

Kelvin placed his arm possessively around my shoulder, and said: 'Well, perhaps not everything'.

They laughed together, I didn't join in.

Maggie turned to her daughter: 'I've put the kettle on, Trude,' then she led the way into the living room and Kelvin followed, pulling me along by the hand. Maggie draped herself on the two-seater and crossed her hair free legs. I chose a single armchair and was pleased to see Kelvin did likewise. Trudie placed a tray of mugs and coffee on the low table and flopped next to her mother.

'Help yourselves, I'm pooped!' She said as she lit up a cigarette.

'Busy day, huh love?' Maggie asked.

'Ah, you can say that again! Everyone started off okay, like they were hiding behind a shield, but they fell apart when they talked. Poor buggers! I mean, families with kids, renting houses, no insurance. How are they going to cope! There's nowhere for them to live ...' Trudie pulled up short.

'Gees, I'm sorry. You two have suffered just as much.'

Maggie patted her daughter's knee.

'No need to apologise love, we'll be okay. I know it's a horrid thing to say, but in some ways it might be good for us.'

We all reached for mugs and poured our coffee in the silence that followed.

Maggie looked at me.

'So, what brings you to Canberra, Fran?'

I almost choked on my coffee. I thought of saying I was passing through.

'She came to see if I was okay,' said Kelvin.

'That's nice.' Maggie sipped her coffee.

Trudie flicked her mother's thigh with the back of her hand. They both spluttered into laughter. I looked at Kelvin in a silent plea for help, but he was smiling too.

'Mum can be so cruel at times. She's joking, Fran!'

Maggie wiped tears of mirth from her eyes with her little finger, carefully avoiding her mascara.

'I'm sorry, Fran. But you should have seen the look on your face! Look, I don't have a problem with you being here. I'm touched that you care enough to have come all this way. I love Kelvin: as the father of my children and as the loyal friend he's always been. But, take him, he's yours!'

She replaced her mug on the tray and stood up.

'Well, I'd better be on my way.'

We all stood up, me with some relief.

Maggie rose on her toes and planted a kiss on her husband's cheek. I looked away, feeling uncomfortable.

"Bye then. I'll let you know when it's all arranged.' Then to me: 'Nice to meet you, Fran. I'll see you around.'

Trudie walked her mother to the front door. Kelvin cupped my chin in his hand.

'Are you okay? Sorry about that, but she insisted on meeting you, to see if I was in safe hands.'

He grinned.

Over dinner that night we discussed the immediate future. The distant future remained a mystery. Trudie suggested that Kelvin and I should "piss off" for a couple of weeks to get away from the horrid memories.

Offices all over Canberra, including Kelvin's, had closed for a fortnight. Most of the workers had been caught up in the fire in one way or another. Those who had not lost their houses were helping out at the recovery centres scattered around the city.

Neither Kelvin nor I could make decisions. I didn't feel it was my place to do so and Kelvin appeared to be flying by the seat of his pants. The solution came from Trudie.

'God! You two are like a couple of teenagers! Sitting there all coy. Fran, take this man to Queensland with you. He can fly back when life's settled down and I'll pick him up from the airport.'

That night, as Kelvin lay beside me, he asked: 'Do you reckon you could put up with an old bloke?'.

'For how long?'

'For as long as we are in love.'

'I reckon I could.'

*****

The drought continued into 1930, and Ellie decided to leave the sheep with Roger at Melvale until things improved. The cattle wandered amongst the trees, eating each green shoot as soon as it sprouted. But despite the hardships, Ellie and her family survived.

Matilda, now four, knew exactly where she fitted in the scheme of things. She accepted that her mother came and went from Grassy Creek, and she now lived with her Aunt Ellie. Whenever Yenohan reappeared, she would take her daughter walkabout for a week or so. When they returned to the homestead, they would speak the language for a few more days until Matilda eased back into the white world.

The day James turned twenty-one, Ellie held a party at Grassy Creek. It was also the day James fell in love with Amanda, the youngest member of the Robinson clan.

The gathering of mostly young people danced among the flowers in the front yard as Stan pumped tunes from his accordion. Mrs Robinson watched her daughter dancing with James and approved. The Thompson's run was a good one, or would be when this damn drought broke, and this good looking young man with black curls would produce strong children.

And so the rift between the Thompsons and the Robinsons closed; particularly since Walter had left for Queensland again and married his boss's daughter.

Nan, who wore her fifty-two years with dignity, stood by Ellie's side watching the two young lovers dancing.

'Does it make you wish you'd married?' she asked Ellie.

'In some ways, yes, but I've never found the right man.'

There was no hint of jealousy or remorse in Ellie's voice. She meant what she said. She did not feel the need to settle for just any man, as did the majority of the young women she knew. Her life was complete. She had her home, her stock, and her child. A husband would simply get in the way. She watched Matilda dance between the adult legs, fascinated by the way the hem of her dress whirled around her. It seemed fitting to Ellie that she should have charge of the child of the only man she had loved.

For the next year, James rode over Pheasant Pass each weekend to court Amanda and returned on Monday to pull his weight at Grassy Creek.

*****

There were few occasions for celebration in the snow belt, so there was much excitement the day James and Amanda married. The tiny stone church at Adaminaby was filled to capacity.

They were all there. The Robinson clan filled the left hand side of the church. Betty Robinson, still round and soft, had made a special effort to look the mother of the bride, and sat amidst her thirteen other offspring, fidgeting with the fussy little hat that kept sliding down her strawberry hair.

Walter eased his tight collar from his Adam's apple and studied Ellie, sitting on the opposite side of the aisle. He coloured at the memory of her rejection, and wriggled closer to his wife.

Jack Swift had even polished his boots. A brown smudge grew on the back of his trouser legs as he continually dusted them. The Davies, complete with Rebecca and Steven, had driven Ellie and Matilda to Adaminaby in their motor car.

James would have asked his brother Joe to be his best man, or his uncle Dan or his uncle Alec. He asked the only other Thompson man still alive, his father.

Roger welcomed this happy intrusion into his staid, predictable life at Melvale. He pushed his tall gangly frame into a three-piece suit, and combed the tangles out of his speckled black and grey beard. He dampened his grey hair and carefully parted it on the side, but after fifty-eight years of going where they willed, the curls sprang back over the parting. He was as happy and proud to be his son's best man as Stan Robinson was to bring his daughter down the aisle to deliver to the safe hands of James Thompson.

Driving home from Adaminaby with the Davies, Ellie stroked Matilda's sleeping head on her knee. She wondered whether she should buy herself a motor vehicle.

After the wedding, Roger stayed with Ellie at Grassy Creek. The newlyweds moved in to Melvale for a couple of months to get used to each other and married life, away from the eyes of their many relatives.

It was the first time Roger had been back to the Boboyan district since leaving seven years earlier. He was proud of his daughter and all she had achieved on the southern lease. Despite the drought years, it was well cared for. All the yards and fences were in good order, and the house was clean and well painted. It had the woman's touch that Melvale now lacked.

Ellie had prepared the leanto bedroom for Roger and she moved Matilda into the front room with her. She noticed Roger never entered the room he had shared with Nola.

'What are you doing about the little one's education?' Roger asked Ellie.

'At the moment I'm teaching her, but I've written to Blackfriars and asked if I can enrol her for next year. It'll be good to have structured lessons, and I can still guide her lessons from here.'

'Good idea,' said Roger.

Time dragged by very slowly for Roger. There were few chores for him to do: chop a bit of firewood, ride around the boundary checking on the fences. The sheep were at Melvale and the cattle weren't ready for mustering.

One day he returned from a visit to the Robinsons leading a one-year-old gelding on a halter. He called for Matilda.

'Here you go, young lady. What do you want to call him?'

Roger winked at Ellie over Matilda's bouncing head.

'Socks!' she said, pointing to his black feet. 'His name is Socks!'

'You hang on to Socks's reins then, and I'll see if I can find you a saddle.'

Roger went to the tackroom and emerged with a lightweight saddle that had belonged to James when he first rode. He threw it over Socks's back, nestled it behind the animal's shoulder, and shortened the stirrup leathers.

'Do you know how to ride?'

Matilda shook her head. Roger lifted her onto the saddle and led Socks around the house yard to let her get the feel of the movement of the horse beneath her, then he flung the reins over its head and showed her how to hold the leather between her thumb and forefinger and loop the trailing rein through her little finger.

'Keep your hands low so's you're not pulling his head up.'

Matilda kicked her heels into Socks's side as she had seen the grownups do, and the quiet little horse moved forward. Matilda gave a yelp.

'Pull on your right hand if you want him to turn right. That's it. Gently now, you don't want him to turn too sharply. Now, pull downwards with both hands to make him stop.'

Socks pulled up obediently. Matilda kicked her heels and they were off again. By dinner time, she had almost full control of her horse. A couple of weeks later, Matilda accompanied Roger and Ellie on a ride to Mount Clear to check on the cattle.

So much had happened that year — the wedding, Roger's prolonged visit to Grassy Creek, Matilda's horse riding lessons — it was only when the wind blew again from the south-west that Ellie realised Yenohan hadn't appeared during Summer. She knew something must have happened to keep Yenohan from Matilda.

*****

Yenohan rode along the banks of the Murrumbidgee River following the sea of woolly backs. She squinted against the bright sun, and pulled the broad brim of her hat over her eyes. They had been on the track for a week now, driving the boss's sheep towards Yass. She should have been riding south at this time of year, towards Matilda, not north, but she had promised her father she would take part in this drive along with his friend, Buckungong.

She eased her stock-whip over her shoulder, and wiped her sweaty palm on her trousers. It would be good to get to Yass and have a decent wash.

She could just make out the upright figure of her father riding ahead of the flock. Beside her, the whistling of Buckungong rose and fell with the lazy rhythm of his horse. Yenohan would have preferred to be riding up front with her father. She hoped she was wrong in suspecting Mudjingal had promised his daughter to his friend.

When they stopped for the night, Yenohan lit the campfire and prepared the damper for the coals. She studied Buckungong as he hobbled the horses. She knew that a woman of thirty shouldn't still be living with her own family, and if she must take a husband, she could do a lot worse than Buckungong. He was in his mid-forties and looking for a woman since the death of his wife. He was a good stockman, never without work even when so many white men were on the Wallaby Track, and he treated her kindly.

Yenohan pulled the damper from the coals then broke off a piece and took it to Buckungong. In the light of the flames, his white teeth smiled in acknowledgment of the meaning of her actions. When they slept that night to the jingling of the horses' hobbles, they lay together.

*****

CHAPTER FOURTEEN

James and Amanda returned to Grassy Creek in the Summer of 1932 with their marriage well established. Roger farewelled his family and returned to Melvale, relieved to be free of the incessant chatter of Matilda, but knowing he would miss her.

Ellie decided to keep the front bedroom for herself and Matilda. She drew comfort from Nola's spirit in the room with the missing ceiling. James moved into the leanto bedroom with his wife and their new double bed. The rats moved back into the old hut which they occasionally shared with strangers who drifted by, seeking the odd job to see them through until things got better.

The entire east coast of Australia had settled into a pattern of low rainfall and unemployment, and the pastures around Boboyan were now no better than those at Melvale. Ellie rode over to Jack Swift's lease along Sheep Station Creek through knee-high brown grass that had not been grazed for years. She had a proposition. Ellie alighted and studied the thin man sitting on his front steps, arms dangling between his knees, a cigarette shielded from the wind in his cupped palm.

'G'day Jack. How's about a cup of tea?'

'Help yourself Ellie. You know where everything is.'

'You want one?'

'Only if it's no bother.'

Jack's was one of the few houses in Boboyan that had a tap over a sink, but the sun didn't shine very brightly through the dusty windows. Ellie waited for the kettle to fill, watching a fly spinning on its back, its legs kicking, trapped in a spider's web. She lifted her eyes to the tumble of weeds shrouding the long forgotten herb garden. This was not a happy home.

Ellie emerged from the kitchen with two mugs and handed one to Jack.

'I've got a proposition for you, Jack. You come and work for me and I'll buy up your lease.'

He looked sideways at Ellie, squinting against the sunlight.

'I don't want your pity Ellie, I'm okay fetching the odd job here and there.'

'It's not pity Jack. I need your grass for my sheep and I need help around the place. And Amanda's pregnant. Now, the way I see it, you could move into the old hut on Grassy Creek and Amanda and

James could take over this house and we could run the sheep on this property.'

Jack looked at the three-roomed weather-board dwelling he had so proudly built when his wife had been expecting Michael. He'd brought in the boards, but he'd cut every roofing shingle himself. He had to admit it was in need of attention.

'I supppose I could. You know Annie's buried here?' said Jack.

'Yes, I do. So does James. They'll look after her grave okay, and you could visit whenever you want.'

Jack held out his hand to Ellie: 'Yeah, go ahead,' and they shook on the deal.

He rose from the steps.

'Better fetch the rum to celebrate then, eh?'

Back at Grassy Creek, Ellie opened the shutters of the old pisé hut and chased the rats away. She repaired the bark roof and sluiced and swept the dirt floor.

Ellie noticed Jack only brought a kit bag with him when he moved in. She wondered if he had left all his memories as she led him to his new home.

'You'll eat in the house with Matilda and me, and I expect a full day's work from you every day except Sundays. You'll need to dress up for Sunday lunch, and wash your hands.'

She turned back to him as she reached the door: 'Oh, and another thing, I would like you to come to Adaminaby with me next week to help me choose a motor vehicle.'

Jack sat on the single bed and looked around the little mud hut. It hugged him, and for the first time in nearly thirty years, he released his wife's ghost.

*****

Matilda squeezed between Ellie and Jack, her legs sideways, carefully avoiding the long gear stick that grew out of the floor. The chug of the V8 motor gently rocked the Ford as Ellie sat in the driver's seat, grasping the steering wheel. She peered past the curved bonnet, awaiting further instructions from Jack. Behind them, the wooden tray was piled with supplies for Grassy Creek.

'Are you sure you want to drive from here, Ellie?'

'Absolutely! You just tell me what to do.'

It wasn't a smooth takeoff, but by the time Ellie had driven her new motor vehicle from Adaminaby to Boboyan she considered herself competent. Jack was impressed with her progress, travelling slowly and carefully over the dirt road, fording the creeks.

She paused at the forty-four gallon drum by the side of the road to collect the mail, then drove to the house paddock and waited for Jack to open the gate. She chugged through, turned off the motor, pulled on the long hand brake and opened the door for Matilda.

James stood on the steps, arms akimbo, smiling at his sister's obvious joy as she wiped the fresh dust from the protruding headlamps. He walked over to inspect the vehicle more closely.

'It must have cost a pretty penny,' said James.

'Three hundred and fifty pounds.'

James let out a soft whistle: 'That would've bought a lot of sheep!'.

'We must move with the times, James. Think of the days we'll save when we go for provisions.'

The mail contained the first of the packages from Blackfriars Correspondence School in Sydney. Matilda's lessons could now begin in earnest.

*****

Ellie had turned a corner of the sewing room over to Matilda's education. Each day for two hours, seated at a small table, Matilda worked through her lessons while Ellie hovered close by, ready for the many questions that came her way. This day they were discussing the notes Matilda's teacher had made on the returned lessons with her red pen, when Matilda suddenly jumped up and ran to the front door as the smell of tobacco wafted through the open window. She wrapped her arms around her mother where the yellow flowers on her skirt changed shape as they stretched across her belly.

Ellie followed Matilda outside and greeted her friend. She ran her hand over Yenohan's stomach: 'You got a husband?'

'Yes Ellie. His name's Buckungong.'

Yenohan's lovely face was radiant with her pregnancy, and at seeing her daughter and friend again. They sat around the kitchen table, like old times.

'Is your mob happy now you've got a black man and having a black baby?'

'Yes, Ellie. So am I. He's a good man, and a good horseman. We work for the boss, taking his sheep to Victoria.'

'Who's your boss?' asked Ellie.

'Mister Cunningham.'

Ellie knew Andrew Cunningham. Two years ago, when he had introduced sheep onto his property at Orroral, he had built a woolshed and had hosted a dance, complete with programme cards, to celebrate its opening. She had also heard the rumour that pastoralists were driving their stock south to Victoria where they were fetching far better prices than those being offered in New South Wales.

'I told Buckungong you are a friend, and said I'd ask if we can stop here for a couple of nights to give the sheep a break. So long as you don't mind. We've put them out on Long Flat.' She grinned at her daughter: ' This way I can spend some time with you, eh Matilda?'.

'Of course you can stay here, Yenohan. Does Buckungong know about Matilda?'

'*No, Ellie. I'll explain that Matilda's your kid. Best we keep him thinking that.*'

That evening Ellie and Matilda joined Yenohan and Buckungong by the campfire beside the creek, laughing and singing. Ellie could see that Yenohan's husband was a kind man, clearly devoted to his wife and forthcoming child. He had no objections when Ellie suggested Yenohan would be more comfortable sleeping in the house for a couple of nights where she curled up with her daughter on the single bed in the lean-to.

The trip to Bairnsdale took four weeks, and sitting in the saddle all day made Yenohan's back ache. The sheep moved slowly, so she spent much of the trip walking, leading her horse. They passed through Jindabyne and Jacobs Ladder, crossed the Snowy River, then entered the State of Victoria and on to the markets, stopping just long enough to prepare for the trip back to their bark-clad hut on Orroral property. This life as the wife of a stockman pleased Yenohan, although nothing would atone for the ache she felt leaving Matilda, and she was at a loss as to how she would be able to see her daughter once her baby was born. They had camped again at Grassy Creek on the way back, but the homestead was deserted.

*****

When Yenohan and Buckungong moved their flock on to Victoria, Ellie drove over to Sheep Station Creek to see James and Amanda. Again, she had a proposition.

'How would you feel about taking the cattle to Bairnsdale this year?' Ellie asked James.

'It's a mighty long way!' He replied.

'Yes, I know that, but it could be worth it.'

'Why ask me, Ellie? You've always made the decisions.'

Ellie looked at Amanda, whose whole attention was given to the small head suckling at her breast.

'It's Matilda. I wondered if she could move in here while we're away. It would be for a couple of months.'

James looked at his wife: 'I don't see why not. What do you think Amanda?'

Amanda stopped stroking the little head and looked up.

'Would you be going too, James?'

'Oh yeah! It's my job!'

'Then I'd welcome her company. She could be a great help with Ruby.'

The following week, Ellie delivered Matilda to her Aunt Amanda, to help care for baby Ruby in exchange for a corner of the kitchen table where she could continue her school lessons, then she joined James and Jack Swift to muster the cattle in Horse Gully. They camped close to where the cattle were feeding and laid out the salt, then rode amongst the largest mob calling out 'S-a-l-l-t!'.

Within a couple of days, most of the cattle had come out of the dense thickets of snow gum into the large drop-log holding yard.

On the third day Ellie, James and Jack entered the less accessible gullies searching for stragglers. At times the terrain was too rough even for the horses, so they took the dogs and walked in. The dogs nipped the heels of the stubborn beasts, flushing them into the open where they were driven to the holding yard ahead of cracking whips. When they had rounded up sufficient beasts, they cut out a hundred of the fattest bullocks for market and drenched the rest before turning them back out to pasture.

Jack resumed his role of camp cook for the duration of the mustering and drive. The Robinsons and the Davies boxed their herds in with the Thompson's at Shannon's Flat, and the combined mob of five hundred began the long drive south.

It took four weeks to get to market, and they met many other herds along the way. But the profits more than paid for the extravagance of owning a motor vehicle.

*****

During the Winter of 1933, Ellie and Jack set a line of a hundred rabbit traps out along the valley. Ellie had no doubt it would be a successful trapping season, the rabbits had taken over the grazing land the previous Summer.

They ran the trap line each morning to collect their harvest, then covered the carcasses with sacks to deprive the waiting currawongs of an easy meal. Ellie sat with Matilda each afternoon to continue her lessons, but Matilda's mind was out in the snow with the birds and the trees.

Jack knew a few tricks about rabbiting. He skinned them cold to get the maximum amount of membrane before stretching them over the wire bow to dry. He packed them at night, head to tail in packs of six, when the skins were heavy with frost. If the weight was good, each skin would fetch a shilling when the rabbit man collected at the end of the Winter.

The weather warmed, and Matilda sat by the creek, singing Wolgal songs, waiting for Yenohan's summer visit.

*****

CHAPTER FIFTEEN

I had been in Canberra two days before it occurred to me to get in touch with my old mate Jill. Perhaps I was in shock too. Jill dragged another chair to her kitchen table for Kelvin. I noticed how tired she looked.

'I'm fine, Fran. Just haven't been sleeping much. The fires missed me by a couple of suburbs, although I did have my computer in the car, ready to leave.'

We left Jill's home and Kelvin drove around so I could see first hand what they had been through. The western side of Canberra bore no resemblance to the neat, well-manicured city I was used to. I kept seeing new sights that shocked: the burnt out shell of the once-proud Mount Stromlo Observatory, its metal frame twisting across the mountaintop; the animal refuge gone; the Equestrian Centre. So many dead animals, so many dead homes.

Before we left Canberra, Kelvin tried to find out the extent of the damage within Namadgi and Kosciusko National Parks, but it was too early for any reliable information to have come through.

Word trickled in that much of the high country had been destroyed and a good many of the huts had been burnt. The KHA updated their web site as losses were confirmed. I cared about all the huts, but it was the unknown fate of Grassy Creek that sickened my stomach.

Then, with the town still in shock, rumours began to spread that the government had not done all it could to prevent the disaster, and hadn't known how to handle it when it arrived. Graziers, who had lived by the motto "grazing prevents blazing", furiously debated the decision made by National Parks to exclude stock, then omit to carry out fuel reduction in the parks.

Full of despair, the people turned on the emergency services and their perceived reticence to send fire crews in earlier.

They needed to blame someone, they needed answers, but I couldn't understand why they turned on the very people who had fought to the point of exhaustion.

*****

In the paradox that is the Australian climate, twenty-five people died in floods in Victoria as drought crippled the rest of the eastern states. Ellie sold off most of the sheep and put all her faith in the cattle.

Everyone cursed the rabbits but relied on their flesh for food and their skins for warmth and income. Ellie and Matilda ran the line of traps each day. James and Jack ringbarked trees to meet the conditions of their lease.

And still Yenohan did not come. Ellie's heart went out to her niece as, each Spring, Matilda watched and waited.

The world was also waiting — for war. Rumours began to spread that, with war imminent, the need for wool would increase, so Ellie brought sheep back onto Grassy Creek and in the Spring of 1938, Ellie, James and Jack drove them up onto Currango Plains for the Summer. This time, twelve-year-old Matilda went too, riding Socks and trailing a packhorse.

From the high plains, the Thompson family watched as a huge black cloud of smoke pushed its way up and over the high mountains to the south. Ash fell from the sky over their stock. Ellie had never been in such a position before, and was at a loss as to what decision to make. Returning to Boboyan would mean travelling towards the fire, and there was no way of knowing how far it had spread; remaining on the endless expanse of dry grass on Currango Plains could be a death trap. For three days they mustered their stock and waited.

Late in the evening of the following Sunday rain began to fall on the western slopes of the Victorian Alps and spread eastwards. Ellie released the stock to feed on the plains again and rode back to Grassy Creek with Matilda to see if they still had a home.

Ellie knew that it was part of the Australian culture to light fires to clean up the country with little regard to the weather. These fires served to clear the scrub for future planting; to get rid of the rubbish under the huge Mountain Ash in case a real fire came through; to kill off snakes; for boundary riders to signal their whereabouts; for graziers to ensure sweet green shoots on their pastures. She was a part of that culture. Ruled by the fear of fire, many settlers protected themselves by tossing a match into their own paddock when they saw a fire approaching.

During the following Winter, Jack and James built a two-stand shearing shed on the rise behind Grassy Creek, beyond the graves, complete with holding yards and a concrete dip. Then they installed a generator in the washhouse to power lead acid batteries and bring 32-volt power to the house.

But the whole valley was still under the cloud of war. Many of the men enlisted, including James. Amanda, angry with her husband, returned to the Robinson household with Ruby.

*****

When next the pipe smoke filled the air, a skinny boy followed Yenohan into the kitchen.

'This's Charlie.'

The name seemed incongruous with the black, black eyes and dark shiny hair, but it was just an outward sign that the Wolgal tribe was losing its identity. Living on Brungle, they were all given white nicknames. Yenohan decided she would spare her son this indignity by naming him in the white man's way from the beginning. Ellie watched Matilda take her half-brother across into the gilgai, showing him all the secret places she had shown Matilda when she was seven. She turned to Yenohan: 'Where's Buckungong?'

'He's gone to war. To New Guinea.'

'So has James. Yenohan, would you be able to stay here? I'm desperate for help.'

'Sure Ellie. I'll stay. I've nothing to go home for without Buckungong there.'

Ellie retrieved the stretcher that was buried beneath years of old tins, and erected it in the corner of the provisions hut for Charlie. Yenohan moved back into the lean-to bedroom with Matilda.

The ewes on Pheasant and Boboyan Hills were near to lambing. Jack hauled water on a slide behind his horse and poured it into the troughs in the lambing paddock, close to the homestead. A week before the ewes were due to lamb, Ellie and Yenohan shepherded five hundred ewes into the secure yard to await the births.

During the daytime, Matilda taught Charlie his lessons as she learnt her own. She had advanced to high school with every intention of becoming a teacher. This was good training.

As the ewes' time approached, the howl of the dingoes drew closer in the evening and the crows roosted nearer to the homestead. Anxiously, Ellie patrolled the ewes.

The first lamb arrived to the waiting beaks of the crows as Ellie, Matilda, Yenohan and Charlie were eating lunch at the kitchen table. By the time they ran to the paddock, Ellie wielding her shotgun, the limp bag of wet wool had gaping holes where it should have had eyes. The ewe lay in a pool of blood, savagely pecked as her lamb had slithered out. Ellie put the muzzle to its head and ended the pain.

With angry tears drying on her face, she dug a hole and buried the pair, then didn't leave the yard for the next three weeks. In the evenings she and Yenohan stayed by the fires, taking turns at sleeping in a swag with one eye open for the sly movement of the dingoes. They helped deliver five stuck lambs, pulling with both hands to help the exhausted ewes. At the end of three weeks, the number of sheep in the yard had doubled.

With all the lambs now born, Yenohan and Matilda did not go to their bedroom, but slipped out under the cover of darkness to the old campsite by Grassy Creek. Yenohan lit the fire the Wolgal way, by flattening a seed stalk of a grass-tree and twirling another, which she had sharpened to a point, between the palms of her hands. The fibres smouldered, then glowed. Matilda spread bark fibres around the hot spot and gently blew a flame to life as Yenohan continued twirling the stalk. Matilda's red hair glowed the colour of the flames as Yenohan stripped her of her white man's clothes and draped a possum cloak over her shoulders.

They talked and sang until first light then silently walked off into Wolgal Country where Matilda learnt which berries made good eating, how to dig for yams, how to prepare kangaroo, koala and porcupine for eating. How to harvest Old Man Weed, boil it up and use it as a remedy for just about every ailment — learning the ways of a Wolgal woman.

*****

Ellie woke to find Charlie sitting alone at the kitchen table, with no sign of Yenohan or Matilda. She went to the old campsite and found the remains of a fire where mother and daughter had sat together through the night, and knew they would be gone some time. She helped Charlie with his lessons, and put him to work in the vegetable patch. She wandered the empty house, lonely and afraid her niece would forget how to be a white woman.

It took three weeks for Yenohan to teach Matilda all she needed to know. When they returned, Matilda's eyes reflected a wisdom that Ellie could not begin to understand, even if Matilda has wished to share it with her. But she wouldn't. She knew, without Yenohan having to tell her, that this special knowledge was not to be shared with white people. Even Aunt Ellie.

That November, for the first time in years, Ellie got a good price for her clip. Britain had entered into an arrangement with Australia to purchase all surplus wool for the duration of the war, and for one full wool season after its completion. The soldiers suffered in the hot, prickly woollen uniforms, but the wool industry prospered.

*****

In 1944, the McKell Labor government was elected during the controversy of the Battle for the Mountain. Parliament passed an act declaring that most of the high leases would become part of Kosciusko State Park. Summer grazing was still permitted in some areas, but Ellie saw the writing on the wall, and decided to end the summer migration of her stock.

James returned from the war to Amanda and Ruby, who were still living with the Robinson household. He felt he was a stranger among these familiar people, especially to the little girl who did not know her father. Amanda had reverted to being a Robinson daughter and, in many ways, James felt the need to court her all over again.

His first task was to drive the sheep to Melvale to allow the pastures in Grassy Creek valley to recuperate. He arrived to find that Roger, at seventy, was struggling to run the property and, like his father before him, was refusing to ask for help from his children. James saw an opportunity of a fresh start with Amanda, away from her large family.

'How would you feel about me and Amanda coming to live here?' he asked Roger. 'Instead of being based in Boboyan and coming north, I could do it the other way around. I'm sure Amanda and Ruby would be happy living in this house.'

Roger smiled at the thought of a lively little girl occupying his days.

*****

PART FOUR

...

CHAPTER SIXTEEN

*M*atilda had never questioned the colour of her skin, not until the year the war ended and she went to college in Sydney. Despite her mother's sporadic visits, which grew more infrequent over the years, she had grown to consider herself a white girl. It therefore came as something of a shock when the other students shunned her because of her Aboriginality.

She studied hard at college through the day and retreated to the safety of Rebecca Davies' small home, where she boarded, in the evening. It was with relief that Matilda returned to Boboyan and began teaching at Shannon's Flat school. Here, away from the suspicion her dusky skin caused amongst the city dwellers, she felt normal.

In the snow belt, a new generation was learning the ropes of the grazing industry. The Robinson's children proved as fruitful as their parents, and their children usually found work in the district. Jack was still a permanent fixture in the old hut at Grassy Creek, but he was stooping with age. Ellie was also beginning to tire and spent her time working the garden or stitching new clothing. Nowadays, she employed the young Robinson men to attend to the sheep and the cattle. During the winters, Matilda spent most weekends with the other young people of Boboyan, skiing across the mountains and camping out in the old deserted tin huts they found on the high plains.

Yenohan was content with her life with Buckungong. Together they drove the boss's cattle and sheep and worked on his property fixing fences. He was a good boss and left them alone to live their lives in the bark hut Buckungong had built in a far corner of the property. Yenohan rode Whisper back to Brungle with Charlie once a year when work was slack. One year, she returned with a heavy cold on her chest that reminded her, unnervingly, of the sickness that had taken Nola Thompson.

*****

While Kelvin waited for reports to come in from Norman and National Parks, I sought out Tilly Anderson whom I had met at Grassy Creek's Open Day.

It had occurred to me that the story of the early settlers should be told. I wasn't sure what I would do with the information, but Tilly was my only link to the Thompsons and Grassy Creek's past.

She lived not far from Trudie, in a house grandly called Melvale. I found it in the middle of an acre of land surrounded by busy roads, set incongruously beside a shopping centre. Tilly walked down the wide concrete stairs to greet me, and the sun picked out the auburn strands among her greying hair. She was pleased to see me.

We sat on the wide verandah trying to make ourselves heard over the constant hum of traffic. She told me how, when she had moved here in 1973, sheep had grazed where the car park now spread. I found this difficult to imagine.

We stepped inside the old house to escape the fumes and din, and into another era. Here, the past had integrity. Family photos hung on either side of the hallway. Photos of modern babies nestled amongst wedding photos of couples whose smiles had been captured a very long time ago. We walked through the lounge with its high pressed-metal ceiling with its ornate rose design atop tongue-and-groove walls.

A three-piece loung curved its well-padded arms in a promise of comfort, protected from greasy heads and hands by antimacassars. A circular rosewood table rested on a single carved leg. There were no unsightly cup rings. I couldn't imagine tea being served without a saucer. No mugs in this house. The kitchen surrounded a large rectangular scrubbed pine table and six bentwood chairs. It was the heart of this home.

Tilly opened the door to the firebox and carefully balanced three pieces of wood, cut the right length, on the glowing coals. She opened the flue and they leapt to life. She pulled a heavy iron kettle forward over the flames.

'It shouldn't take too long.'

Steam was already rising from the spout.

'What brings you back to Canberra, Fran?'

'I was worried about the fires.'

'I thought it might have had something to do with that lovely man. Kelvin? Was that his name?'

I smiled.

'Well, yes. I was worried about him too.'

'He genuinely cares about the old homestead. Him and Norman. They took the time to track me down and ask me all sorts of questions before they started fixing it up. They mostly got it right. Not the kitchen though, they didn't get that right. They forgot to put in the fuel stove, but I can forgive them for that. Everything else is much how it used to be.'

Tilly poured hot water into the teapot and covered it with a red and green ribbed knitted cosy. She continued: 'They don't know whether Grassy Creek survived the fires. I rang Parks but could only leave a message. I guess they're too busy at the moment to return calls. It'll break my old heart if it's gone, Fran.'

As she reached up to lift two cups from the hooks I noticed a framed picture on the dresser. A young girl about five years old balanced on her right foot between a white woman and an Aboriginal woman, her left foot tucked behind her knee. They were all dressed up in their Sunday best, holding hands, smiling at the camera.

'Who are they?' I asked.

She picked up the photo and placed it on the table.

'That's me in the middle, and that's my mother and Aunt Ellie.'

'Was your Aunt Ellie from the local tribe?'

'It's the other way around. My mother is Yenohan, the black woman.'

I felt embarrassed. It took some rethinking to reverse my assumptions.

'My mother was a Wolgal woman. She'd be a hundred and three if she was still alive. Aunt Ellie was my father's sister. She brought me up.'

I sipped my tea, waiting for Tilly to tell me more.

'My mother and Aunt Ellie were friends since they were kids. Then, when Mum was about eighteen, the Board tried to tell her to go and work for some white fella she didn't know. Nola — that's Aunt Ellie's mother — came to the rescue and put her to work around the homestead, cleaning and cooking for the men.

'That's how she got to know Joseph, my father. Mum never talked about him. I only know what Aunt Ellie told me. But I gather he and Mum kept their love a secret from their families. Scared of what they'd say, a black woman with a white man.'

'Didn't you know your father?'

'No. He died before I was born. He was thrown by his horse. Probably spooked by a snake, there were lots of tigers up there.'

'How come your aunt brought you up, then?'

'I was born at Brungle Mission Station. The manager tried to tell Yenohan that the Tribe wouldn't want me: a girl with red hair. The government men wouldn't let her alone, either. Mum was scared the police would take me away, so she took me to Grassy Creek and more or less handed me over to Aunt Ellie. It must have hurt Mum, but she thought that if she could leave me with the Thompsons, I would be with part of my family. As it turned out, Aunt Ellie was only too pleased to take me in. She'd been close to her brother, and she wasn't married. Didn't have kids of her own. Yenohan came back and visited from time to time and took me into the bush. I'm real lucky, Fran. Even though I live life as a white woman, I know about the Aboriginal ways.'

'What happened to Yenohan?' I asked.

'Once Aunt Ellie took over my upbringing, Yenohan was trapped between two worlds. Whenever she was with her family, she missed me, and worried about me. But when she was at Grassy Creek, she felt she had lost her daughter to a white woman and she missed her family. She eventually married a man from Brungle. They had a boy,

Charlie. He's a cultural officer with Parks. He visits me when he's in Canberra.'

Tilly took the teapot to the stove and topped it up.

'So you stayed on at Grassy Creek?' I asked.

She bought the pot back to the table and filled my cup.

'Yes. When I was twenty-one I married George. He was a local lad. He called me Tilly, but my real name is Matilda. We took over Grassy Creek when we had Frank, our son. Aunt Ellie reckoned we needed the house to ourselves and so she moved up here to Melvale to live with her brother, James and his family. There's a lot more room in this old house.'

'Was Roger Thompson still alive then?'

'He was getting on a bit. Seventy-seven. He had a lot to do with Aunt Ellie deciding to move up here. But he only lasted another year. He was happy, though. He loved having all the family around him.'

'You've got a grandson, haven't you?'

Tilly got up from the table and lifted another photo down from the dresser. A father and son, both with red hair and brown eyes, smiled from the frame.

'And a great-grand-son! That's Michael, and the young'un is David.'

'I remember seeing them at the open day.'

Tilly placed the photo on the table beside the photo of herself. The family resemblance was strong.

'Open day. All those people were wandering through my home as if it was some sort of museum. I still find it painful to return there. You know, even after all this time, this place isn't home. Home will always be Grassy Creek. George and Frank ran that place like clockwork, even after Frank married Tracy. She was no good. Ran off, leaving us with the little 'un.'

Tilly's mind sprang back to the present: 'I didn't thank you for caring for me during the open day. For helping me escape the crowd. It meant a lot to have someone who understood how sacred that place is to me.'

As we hugged our farewell, I promised I would let her know the minute I heard news of Grassy Creek.

*****

The old horse struggled up the mountainside, his legs quivering, pawing at the soft snow, seeking purchase. He was long past the age when a horse would expect to lead a dignified life of retirement in a quiet paddock — or be shot. But he was cherished and his spirit remained keen.

His grey muzzle hung low as Yenohan slid from the saddle and clung to the pommel, waiting for a coughing spasm to pass. She spat a ball of pink froth onto the white snow. She dropped the reins to the ground and crept into the hut.

Squatting by the fireplace, Yenohan loaded her pipe and lit it before throwing the match onto a bundle of twigs. They spluttered, smoked, then caught. She fed the fire and waited for it to warm her aching lungs.

*****

The sun shone warmly on Matilda's face. She leant against the verandah post, knowing herself lucky that she, a redhead, could take the sun without burning.

She chewed the end of her pencil for inspiration as she prepared the lessons for her school children. Matilda was a dedicated teacher, like her grandmother, Nola, before her. She laid her pad and pencil aside and began to cut star shapes from a sheet of red cardboard. She liked to encourage her students with rewards to paste on the border of their slates.

A truck drew up to the house gate and Matilda smiled as she rose to greet the young man who climbed down from the cab. George Anderson had moved to Boboyan as the war ended, and had bought the old Swift property from her Aunt Ellie. Matilda encouraged his courtship.

Matilda and George walked towards the house, his arm around her waist.

'Is there someone on Mount Clear?' He asked.

Matilda looked back to where George was pointing and noticed a thin column of smoke rising, halfway up the mountain.

'Not as far as I know. How strange.'

As the afternoon progressed, the smoke became thicker. Ellie walked from the clothes line carrying a laundry basket and Matilda drew her attention to the smoke.

'It must be a stockman passing through,' said Ellie. But she was puzzled. The old slab hut hadn't been used since the thirties, and it was not on any stock route.

'If it's still going in the morning, we'll ride up and take a look.' Ellie turned to George.

'Are you staying for tea, George?'

'No thanks, Ellie. I'm returning some books I borrowed from the school teacher here. I'd best be getting back.'

Ellie carried the washing inside and lit the chip heater ready for a long hot soak in the tub. George kissed Matilda's cheek and bounded back to his truck.

At daybreak the next day, there was no sign of smoke from Mount Clear and the two women went about their chores. At morning tea on the front verandah, Jack helped himself to a scone: 'Someone's on Mount Clear. Saw the chimney smoking yesterday arvo.'

They looked toward the mountain and once again saw a thin spiral of smoke wafting into the clear winter sky.

'I'll go up after lunch and see what's what,' said Matilda.

Socks scrambled up and over the rocky climb then through the forest of peppermint gum and emerged at the bottom of the steep slope below the old slab hut.

The white ants had done their work on the saplings under the verandah roof, causing it to lean unsteadily to the left. The door was open, and Whisper stood outside, his head hung low. Matilda dismounted and walked over to stroke the familiar grey muzzle.

'Are you still alive, old fella? Where's Yenohan?'

Matilda heard a rasping cough from inside the hut. She entered the dark interior. It smelt of animal dung and tobacco. A bundle of blankets stirred by the hearth. Matilda bent over and gently brushed aside the black and grey speckled curl that hung over her mother's eyes. A thin hand held onto the young arm and the hut was filled with laboured breathing.

Yenohan opened her eyes, milky brown irises floating in a sea of pink. She propped onto an elbow and foraged for her pipe. She drew on it, her lungs gurgling with the effort, then she looked at her daughter.

'Breaks me heart to see that red hair of yours, girl. You look so like your dad.'

'Why have you come, Yenohan?' Matilda said, soothingly.

'I want to die in Wolgal Country, not Brungle. And I've been thinking about Joe. I want to die here too.'

'Are you sure you're going to die?'

'Yes, girl, I'm sure. Brungle doc say it's me lungs. I've been mighty sick.' She couldn't continue for coughing.

Matilda went outside and combed the yard for thick branches and built the fire to a roar, then unwrapped Yenohan's sweating figure from the blanket. She removed her stiff moleskins and unbuttoned the flannelette shirt. Yenohan's breasts flopped sideways like pieces of string over her skinny ribs. Matilda could not believe that in just a few years, Yenohan had gone from a healthy woman to this.

Matilda soaked her handkerchief in water from her bottle and cleansed Yenohan's body of the grime accumulated from her long ride back to Wolgal Country. Yenohan didn't object. Matilda held the bottle to Yenohan's parched, scaly lips, and her pink tongue licked at the fluid.

'We'd better get you down to the homestead,' said Matilda.

'No girl. No time. I wouldn't make it. I want to stay here with Joe.' She closed her eyes and drifted somewhere between sleep and unconsciousness.

Matilda wrapped Yenohan in the blanket again, checked on the fire, then rode back to Grassy Creek as fast as the snow allowed.

Ellie was in the kitchen when Matilda dashed in. Grabbing clean clothes, towels, washers, food, she jammed them into her saddlebag.

'It's Yenohan. She's up there and she's dying.'

Ellie saddled Freckles and hurried after her niece.

It took two days for Yenohan to die her awful death. She called Matilda Joe. She called Ellie Nola. But through it all, she smiled as her daughter crooned Wolgal songs.

*****

CHAPTER SEVENTEEN

Matilda knew there were strangers approaching by the way the dogs barked. She parted the lace curtains and saw a Land Rover, with a government crest on the door, stop outside the house gate. Three men emerged.

George stopped working on the tractor engine in the garage and picked up an old towel from the mudguard to wipe his hands. He brought the three border collies to heel with a sharp whistle, and they wriggled under the house to resume their midday sleep.

'G'day,' said George, from the doorway. 'What can I do for you?'

The driver reached inside the cab and lifted his hat from the dashboard, then shook George's hand. He wore a short-sleeved shirt and tie, as did his two companions.

'Tom Draft. This is Eddie Smart and Jeff Simpson. You'd be George Anderson?'

'Yeah, that's right.'

'Well, George, we've a spot of surveying to do in the area. We'll probably be around here for a couple of weeks. Just wondering if we could bunk down in the shearing quarters, if it's no trouble. There'll be other blokes around too, working over in the next valley.'

'Sure, make yourselves at home.'

There was nothing unusual about passers-by using the quarters.

'What are you surveying?' said George, as he led the way over the rise to the bunkhouse.

'It's a government thing. You know what they're like: always need to know where everything is.' Tom Draft gave a hollow laugh.

George swung open the unpainted door: 'She's rough, but she should do'.

'Thanks, George. Much appreciated. We'll try not to get in the way too much.'

George returned to the waiting tractor. It didn't occur to him to question any further.

The Anderson's grandson was thrilled to have these men staying around his house. He followed them everywhere, asking all sorts of questions that the men cheerfully answered: how high up was their house? — over four thousand feet; what was the temperature each morning? — twenty-five degrees Fahrenheit; could he have a ride in the Land Rover ...

The three men finished their work and disappeared, leaving the shearers' quarters tidy and the generator full of diesel. Life returned to normal and the Andersons forgot about their visitors.

Six months later, in the Summer of 1972, odd things started to happen in the Boboyan district. Yellow cement posts with bold red numbers appeared. Rumours spread: the government was marking out the leases — although the yellow posts did not align with any boundaries; the whole of Naas valley would be flooded to supply water for the rapidly-growing city of Canberra; the entire territory was destined to become a national park.

Frank Anderson told his mother and father to ignore the rumours: this property had belonged to the Thompson family for nearly a hundred years, and they weren't about to lose it. But as he watched his own son running freely around the house paddock, he wasn't so sure.

It was only when Matilda opened the letter from the Department of Services and Property that she finally knew they would lose Grassy Creek.

Mr G Anderson

You are advised that the freehold lands owned by E & J Thompson, and M & G Anderson were formally acquired by the Commonwealth on 26 July 1973.

Papers relating to the acquisition will be forwarded to the Deputy Crown solicitor in a few days. That office will be in contact with you regarding settlement for the lands.

Yours Sincerely

JJ Mule

Acting Chief Property Officer

George walked into the kitchen and saw the look on his wife's face. He took the letter from her shaking hands.

'What's this then, eh?'

He slowly sank onto the bentwood chair as he read the letter.

*****

The creek rushed past the grassy mounds, drawing minute specks of silt into its waters to deposit them further downstream and begin the process of building new mounds. It had been a good year. The rain had fallen as and where it was needed. The creek continued on through the wet gully past the lyrebirds practising their repertoire. Some time ago they had added another verse to their song: the throb of a diesel generator. Beyond the creek, buttercups and purslane were starting to bloom, and yellow billy buttons fought the snow daisies for a tenuous toehold on the spongy sphagnum moss of the gilgai.

Corroboree frogs stretched their legs and lungs in the spring air and striped skinks flicked their tails in the warm sunshine, seeking out smooth rocks upon which to bask. A bogong moth flew into a crevice of an ancient rock and suspended its furry body, awaiting the arrival of its brothers. White cockatoos wheeled through the trees, gathering on the branches of a tall snow gum before playfully tumbling and filling the air with their raucous song. A gentle breeze puffed the powdery new leaves of the black sallee, fanning the kangaroo stretching in its shade, its eyes partly closed. The sun appeared over Mount Clear to the east, chasing the shadows of the mountains back towards their foothills as it had done since the beginning of time.

But no cattle wandered over Boboyan or Pheasant Hills. The yards in front of the shearing shed stood empty.

Matilda Anderson closed the front door for the last time. She felt numb. She unhooked the weathered board with the words "Grassy Creek" burnt into it, and hurled it into the back of the ute along with the rest of the last minute items. She climbed into the cab where her grandson waited. She gripped the steering wheel and leaned her head on her hands to lessen its throb.

George and Frank had left the day before to truck the cattle and sheep to Melvale.

'Gran, will Fluffy be alright in the back?' Her grandson's voice crackled with emotion. Matilda lifted her head and turned the key. The diesel sluggishly came to life.

'Yeah, Fluffy'll be okay. He's in his basket. Don't worry.'

She backed the ute out of the yard, past the vegie garden that Nola had started sixty-five years before. It had never disappointed the Thompson family since. She left the gate open; let the roos and rabbits have their fill.

'Gran, did we pack my dominoes?' The most important lesson Michael had learnt in this, his first year at school, was the game with the black and white tiles.

'You checked yourself. There's nothing left.'

Nothing but memories and graves.

Matilda drove the whole distance from Grassy Creek to Melvale in a daze. She stopped for Michael to hop onto the galvanised pipe gate and swing it open, as he always did, then race the ute along the long dusty driveway to the wide concrete stairs.

Hooves clattered impatiently against the sides of the stock trucks and the smell of stale manure hung heavily in the air. Bullocks bellowed and sheep bleated from within their prisons. Ellie rose from the squatter's chair to greet her niece. She felt the pain that was Matilda's.

Matilda sat on the verandah beside Ellie, and spoke of her deepest worry: 'Will they look after the graves?'

'I do hope so, my dear. Both our mothers are buried there. And your father, my brother. I'm sure the government means no harm. They're only doing it to protect the land. That's what they say, anyway.'

'Protect it from what?' Matilda didn't try to hide the bitterness in her voice. Here she was, not yet fifty, and she felt her life was over. 'We looked after that land!'

'You don't need to convince me, dear.'

'You wait! Without the animals to keep the grass down, it'll become overgrown. No trickleburn, it'll be a death-trap. You mark my word!'

Ellie patted Matilda's knee: 'I'll go and start dinner'. She heaved herself from the low-slung canvas chair and went inside, she moved a lot slower than she used to. She remembered how Nancy had crept around the house with her shawl dangling from her shoulders. She had thought her seventy-year-old grandmother so old. Ellie was now seventy-three.

Matilda remained outside as the long shadows covered the sunlight on the paddock. A carpet of dried leaves beneath the gums took on a golden glow as if they were lit from below, from within the earth itself.

It was well after dark when George joined his wife on the verandah. He wanted to comfort her, but he knew her anger was strong.

'It'll be okay, Tilly. We'll make it work here. Melvale's a good property.'

Ellie called them in for tea. Matilda shook a handkerchief from the pocket of her jeans and blew her nose.

'You go in George. I'm not hungry.' Her blocked nose muffled her words.

George ruffled his wife's short auburn hair.

'Don't catch cold out here.'

A three-quarter moon lit the wide paddocks surrounding Melvale; the same moon that flooded Grassy Creek valley with its silver glow as a masked owl began to clean out her nest in the hollow of a dead mountain ash.

For a long time Matilda sat musing over the resumption of the land; the same land that had been lost to her mother's Wolgal people so long ago, and now had been taken from her father's people. She felt that she, a mixture of Wolgal and Thompson, had lost out twice.

*****

(1986)

Rain pelted down, silver dashes as it passed before the bank of headlights, adding to the already swollen creek. A young man peered through the windscreen of his ute, his muscled arms working the steering wheel as the vehicle bounced and rattled over the rocks hidden amongst the clumps of grass. His companion pulled a red-checked flannelette shirt over his navy singlet, then replaced his baseball cap.

'Fuck!' They shouted in unison, then laughed as the vehicle slewed sideways in a slippery patch of black mud. Two broad-chested dogs, one golden brindle the other beige, braced themselves as they dug their claws into a square of carpet tied onto the bonnet. Their balance was good.

The ute passed a clump of blackberries and both dogs catapulted from the bonnet into the tangle of thorns and fruit. A pig darted from the opposite side and ran for its life. The two men whooped with glee and zigzagged after the pig and the dogs. The pig ran past the solitary homestead, through the tumble-down fence, and backed into a huge old snow gum, facing the dogs. The ute ground to a stop and the driver aimed the headlights at the base of the tree, then grabbed his Winchester from the dashboard. The man in the flanny closed his fist around the hilt of a knife in his belt and waited for his dogs to do their work.

The two dogs, each protected by thick leather breastplates, dodged the flashing tusks and made for the pointed ears. The pig flicked back and forth, charging one dog, then the other.

But the pig didn't stand a chance. As the dogs sank their powerful teeth into its ears and held fast, the man in the flanny approached from behind and grabbed its hind legs. He rolled the pig onto its side and bound its kicking legs together, then sunk his knife deeply into its throat and pulled downwards through the coarse black hair on its belly. The pig's legs were still kicking as pink and grey entrails spilled from the slit and the dogs snatched at their reward. The driver enthusiastically blasted the ute's horn then ran, splashing through the mud, to the bloody scene.

'Fuck, man, that's a corker of a porker. Gotta be ninety kilos.'

The pig lay in its own blood, its ears missing, its snout chewed to a pulp. The two men pulled the dogs from the body and dragged the pig by the hind legs over to the truck and suspended it from a frame above a wire cage beside six carcases, dressed and ready for the chiller.

'Let's get out of this fucking rain,' said the driver, and reached inside the cab to turn off the headlights. His overalls were caked with mud and blood. He whistled the dogs and ran to the homestead, kicking the door open with his heavy leather boot. The screws of the bottom hinge let go the rotting timber and the door dangled by its top hinge. The man with the flanny darted to the ute and lifted a slab of beer onto his shoulder then, as an afterthought, grabbed a jerrycan of petrol. Inside, he chucked a beer to his mate.

'Get this inside you.'

'We need a fire, that's what we need.'

'Thought of that,' and he sat the jerrycan near the fireplace.

They looked around for firewood, then the driver walked through the door into another room and began prising loose floorboards with his pig spike.

'Plenty more where this come from,' and threw them in the fireplace. His mate sloshed petrol from the jerrycan onto the planks before flicking his cigarette lighter. They removed their wet clothes and hung them by the fire to dry.

The Grassy Creek fireplace had never known such a fierce fire. Flames licked the wall above the mantelpiece, scorching the boards; they leapt high, beyond the top of the chimney. The mortar that had held the stones in place for seventy-five years dried and began to loosen its grip.

In the grey dawn, the two men stumbled from the hut with heads like thunder. The dogs bounded onto the carpet-draped bonnet, ready to find their next pig.

****

In the Spring of 1995, a group of people waded across the water of Grassy Creek to inspect the homestead. Norman had brought some members of KHA to assess the sad wreck. A forty-four gallon drum leaned at an angle against the verandah post, slowly rusting into the ground.

The sun concentrated its brilliance on a jagged edge of glass protruding from the chewed red cedar window frame, flashing for a moment as if it were a diamond. Bullet holes peppered the southern wall.

Norman clambered over the pile of rocks that had once been a chimney and entered the building through the hole they had left. Stepping carefully over the missing floorboards, he noticed black soot fanning out from the fireplace surround. He wondered why the whole place hadn't burnt to the ground years before.

He sank onto the front steps. He hated these moments between despair and action .He pulled his notebook from his pocket and began to document the damage.

****

CHAPTER EIGHTEEN

The further north we drove, the more Kelvin relaxed. The perpetual frown across his forehead smoothed and his eyes danced. He became playful. He hummed to the wind as it rushed through the car window to toy with his hair. He was no longer an old bloke.

By the time we reached Brisbane he was a very different person from the one I had known for the past nine months. The fire and the fate of the huts retreated to the back of our minds.

The older parts of Brisbane are very hilly. Paddington is no exception. It has become a trendy suburb for the young people of Brisbane to gather at coffee shops on Sundays and share the morning's newspapers.

Its streets, built for horse and buggy, are narrow and the allotments are small. Most of the houses, built around the end of the nineteenth century, have front steps leading straight from the footpath to the front door. I proudly led Kelvin into my worker's cottage — lovingly restored, mostly by myself. He was amused to find that Queensland houses actually did stand on stilts.

Because my allotment slopes away so steeply from the road, my house, at street level in the front, stands three metres tall at the back. I took Kelvin underneath to show him my six dining room chairs. They were finished, except for the tapestry seat covers I was stitching in front of the television each evening.

He ran his hands over the smooth slim curves, admiring my work.

'I've got just the table to go with these,' he said.

I didn't know if I was supposed to have heard this news. I waited for him to continue.

'I almost lost it in the fire.'

A haunted look revisited his eyes.

'I only had minutes to grab what was important when the final rush came. A whole lifetime's memories were in that house, and I grab a table! It was then I realised that the future with you was what mattered, not the past. I knew the kids had photos of their childhood.'

He pulled me to him and sighed.

'I'd have looked a fool if you'd have said no, wouldn't I?'

'You must have known there was no danger of that.'

'I was pretty sure.'

The following night was my monthly folk club. My friends hugged Kelvin as I introduced him. He would have to get used to hugging hairy men. In the glow of candlelight in an old brick hotel we listened to my friends sing and recite their way through the evening. I knew this scene was foreign to Kelvin.

We all arranged to go bush-walking in the mountains of Binna Burra the next day to show Kelvin the magic of the temperate rain forests in the rugged border ranges between Queensland and New South Wales. I was showing off as I knew he would not have experienced such a forest around Canberra.

Kelvin, in his element and his boots, walked around the Antarctic Beech trees, spellbound by their ancient knotted roots clothed in mosses, dripping in the swirling mist. We ate our lunch on the edge of a bluff, dangling our feet in New South Wales. The mountain ranges before us rivalled those of the high country. Kelvin almost forgave me for introducing him to leeches.

During the following week I took him to the Queensland Art Gallery to share my favourite paintings, then we lunched at a small cafe, watching the city buildings reflected in the Brisbane River. I showed him the Muttaburrasauris fossil in the Queensland Museum; we strolled in the old Botanical Gardens, climbing among the roots of the ancient Banyans as if we were children. We rode the Citycat ferry down the Brisbane River in the evening as the lights from the skyscrapers danced over the ripples in our wake and watched climbers abseiling down the floodlit cliffs of Kangaroo Point.

And every night we made love.

No longer confined to a small tent or needing to be quiet in Trudie's home, the whole house was ours: the bed, the bath, the woolly rug in the living room, even the back deck at 3:00 am under a balmy sky full of stars.

Then, one evening, as we curled up on the couch watching telly, the phone rang.

'Fran? Hello, it's Norman here. How are you, girlie? Looking after that man of yours, I hope.'

'Yup. Keeping him fed and watered.'

'And happy?'

'Oh yes, we're very happy.'

'Can I speak to him?'

I handed Kelvin the phone: 'It's for you.'

The week's relaxation fled from his face as he walked outside with the hand piece. Only a handful of people knew where he was. This call could only mean trouble.

Kelvin hung up the phone and joined me in the living room.

'We've lost ninety per cent of Namadgi.'

We allowed the magnitude of this news the silence it deserved.

'What about Grassy Creek?' I asked, not really wanting to hear the answer.

He visibly lightened: 'It's okay. So are Demandering and Horse Gully. But four huts have been burnt.'

'Gee, that's not too bad considering ...'

'It gets worse. Seventy per cent of Kosciusko's burnt. We've lost nineteen huts there, and twenty-four in Victoria. Over a million hectares gone. And the fires are still burning.'

I picked up the phone and rang Tilly's number.

Virtually all the High Country of Australia had been burnt, some of it never to recover. The soil was sterile for a metre below the surface, no seeds could survive such an environment. The nature of the Australian High Country had changed forever.

In Canberra alone, the fires had claimed four lives, four hundred and seventy-five houses, and a whole generation of animals. The government predicted it would take a minimum of three years just to complete a survey of the damage.

But heroic stories started to emerge of national park officers who had landed their helicopters to back burn around some of the huts, then continued on to fight the fire.

As soon as it was safe to do so, the Parks guys had taken Norman for a ride in their helicopter. As president of the Kosciusko Huts Association, it was his right to see the damage first hand.

The whole of the Murrumbidgee Valley was blackened, but the Boboyan corner of Namadgi National Park had been spared. Grassy Creek, Naas Creek and Sheep Station Creek still looked the same.

It was obvious our week of bliss had come to an end.

'I'd better get back,' said Kelvin. 'Norman'll need a hand preparing a report for Parks. He's already making noises about a hut replacement policy.'

We talked through our last night until dawn.

'Where do you picture us living?' asked Kelvin.

'There's no question about that,' I replied. 'I have no ties up here. And I hate the heat. You have family and a job in Canberra. Besides, I've always secretly wanted to live there.'

'Are you sure?'

'Absolutely.'

'What about all your friends up here? They're a lovely crew, even if they do smoke dope.'

I laughed: 'Oh sure, I'll miss them, but we all get together at the folk festivals, so we'll catch up. Besides, I've lots of folkie friends in Canberra too. It'll be nice to spend more time with them.'

'Then, how soon can you move down?'

'How soon can you find us a house?'

'Maggie's in the process of fixing up about the insurance. As soon as that's settled, we'll take half each and start life again. It was a smart house, worth quite a lot. We should be able to buy a comfortable, if more modest, house with my share.'

'Then I'll put this house on the market tomorrow, and come down as soon as it's sold.'

'Do you have to wait till it's sold?'

'Probably not.'

'That's my girl.'

I drove Kelvin to the airport and a month later saw my worldly possessions, including six completed red cedar dining chairs, onto a moving van. With a modicum of sadness I closed the door on my past, and followed the van south, driving through torrential rain that would put an end to the dreadful fires of 2003.

*****

ABOUT THE AUTHOR

Dale Lorna Jacobsen is a freelance writer who has the good fortune to live in the bush just outside Maleny in the Hinterland of the Sunshine Coast. She is passionate about grass-roots history which led to the publication of three novels: *Union Jack* (2011), political intrigue set in Queensland in the 1920s; *Yenohan's Legacy* (2013), a story of love and life in the High Country of Australia, *Being Lucy* (2018), the story of a mountain recluse set in East Gippsland.

In 2013 she fulfilled a life-long dream, taking part in an expedition to Antarctica, and produced an eBook, *Why Antarctica? a Ross Sea odyssey* (2015). Dale has since returned twice to Antarctic.

Web: https://www.dalelornajacobsen.com
Facebook: https://www.facebook.com/dalelornajacobsenauthor

9 780648 578611